Cousin Anne

A Prequel to
Pride and Prejudice

Also by Diane H. Morris
Rosings Park

The *Surgeon's Duty* series:

Ravaging the Dead
Naught but Butchers
No Hallowed Ground

Read the author's blog at
www.moorgatebooks.com
for information about
medicine, childbirth, inheritance and
the lives of women during England's
Regency period:

There's a Leech for That!
Mr. Darcy Was a Second-Class Citizen
Linseed Tea: Popular in Jane Austen's Day and Today
It Is a Truth Universally Acknowledged
Man-Midwives Behaving Badly
Why Isn't Mr. Darcy a Lord?

Cousin Anne

Diane H. Morris

Moorgate Books
Knoxville, Tennessee

Cousin Anne is a work of fiction. Names, characters, places, and
incidents either are the product of the author's imagination or
are used fictitiously. Any resemblance to actual events or persons,
living or dead, is entirely coincidental.

Printed in the United States of America

www.moorgatebooks.com

Cover design by CreateSpace

ISBN (paperback) 978-1-941033-02-9
ISBN (Kindle) 978-1-941033-04-3
ISBN (eBook) 978-1-941033-06-7

Library of Congress Control Number: 2015915280

For Mum, a true treasure

Chapter 1

A Troubling Diversion

"I hope you aren't reading anything inappropriate."

At these words Anne looked down the length of the library to where her cousin Fitzwilliam Darcy stood near the fireplace clutching a fire iron.

"Not at all," she said lightly. "I have here several perfectly ordinary books."

She picked up one. "I have been reading Dr. Hill's *Virtues of British Herbs*, which discusses the common coltsfoot, of which the Rosings cook is so fond. I did not know that it's used to treat consumption and inflammation of the kidneys."

She touched a book on top of a short stack. "Dr. Pulteney's *Sketches of the Progress of Botany in England* contains a biography of Sir Hans Sloane, whose Jamaican collection forms the basis of the British Museum. Miss Waygood and I hope to visit its collection while we are in Town. And I discovered this book on the Syrian city of Aleppo—a fascinating review that contains several delightful engravings."

She waved a hand over her hoard. "Surely these must be acceptable."

He nodded his approval. "It is good you choose to avoid last spring's situation."

"Oh, yes. I have learned my lesson." She smiled like a simpleton until he sat down, after which she squinted at the back of his head. Her scowl would scare an infant.

Of course she remembered the trouble she'd caused when her uncle Darcy caught her reading *Aristotle's Compleat Master Piece*. Her uncle had spluttered and ranted and berated her for unladylike conduct. "I am deeply displeased, shocked even," he had said, "to find you reading a text not fit for any respectable young lady."

She had resigned the book into his hands, apologized for offending him, and told him she had only chosen it out of curiosity and not read much beyond the preface. He was prepared to believe her.

She decided not to explain that she was reading it through a second time.

How could she not be fascinated by Aristotle's question: Why shouldn't the mysteries of nature regarding the generation of man be studied without blame? Nature has no need to be ashamed of any of her works, the great philosopher had written, and for this reason Anne felt no shame reading about virginity and copulation and about the male yard and stones and the seat of lust in women.

Nor did she fear her father's censure. After all, the popular book had been circulating for forty years or more.

When Sir Lewis de Bourgh had been told of her exploit, he appeared somewhat careless of his parental duties, for he failed to reprimand or guide her, which only irritated and confused uncle Darcy.

Anne herself wondered where her uncle would hide the book when his own daughter, Georgiana, grew old enough to be interested in one of Nature's great secrets.

On this dreary November morning she knew to be careful. Sinking behind her wall of books she resumed her study of an unwieldy, cloth-bound tome every bit as forbidden as Aristotle's. She stared at the creature fixed in awful splendor on a yellowing page. A brazen anatomist had sliced through its mother's belly and stripped the shredded tissue to reveal the hidden gem snug within its shell—a perfectly formed child.

The dissection was a sacrilege, an affront to every feeling person, but the engraving inspired awe. Her finger traced the child's arm. Surely cherubs had shaped its bulbous body and bunched fingers; surely angels formed its bent foot and perfect ear. She wondered what misstep, what cruel fate, had stolen its life. She marveled at the draftsman whose steady hand sketched its gruesome beauty. She struggled to read the Latin inscription—for what purpose she could not say, except that doing so made her happy.

So lost was she in this supernatural world that the chatter of maids in the hall and the raucous call of a coach driver barely reached her. Only when Fitzwilliam stirred in his wing-back chair near the windows did she pause. Knowing he would not approve of her course of study, she remained skittish and furtive, else he discover her guilty pleasure.

The gloomy shadows lengthened. The room grew chilly.

Anne worked undisturbed, cocooned, until the door opened, at which sound she looked up.

A well-dressed young man stood on the threshold, a wry grin on his face. He pulled the door closed and went to the bookshelves as though searching for a beloved story to beguile away the time.

Anne bent her head as if in concentration, her ears alert to his movements.

Careless of his rustlings, the youth made his way down the long line of bookcases, selecting first this tome, then that one, next another one. None of them held his attention for more than a few heart beats. Finally he arrived at a point behind Anne's chair. Holding a book chosen at random he leaned over and said in low tones, "You need a diversion, cousin. Shall I conjure one for you?"

Anne felt the breathy invitation tickle her ear. She closed her book and laid her arms across its cover. "What do you have in mind?" she whispered. In George Wickham's deep-set brown eyes she found mischief lurking. He looked every bit a rogue and might as well be nine years old as the nineteen years she knew him to be. "Will it make me laugh?"

His lips puckered—a challenge. "No doubt of it."

"You look like trouble. Have you planned a disturbance?"

"A disturbance!" he cried with mock seriousness, placing a hand over his heart. "Why would you ask such a question?"

"Surely you can guess why I might inquire about your intentions. You can settle to nothing and have been haunting the library like a ghost this past quarter-hour."

"Oooooh," he crooned, sounding more like a sick hound than a phantom, which made Anne snicker in an unladylike manner. "That is better. You are far too serious for a young lady of fashion. One would think you were preparing to enter Cambridge. What are you reading?" He reached over as if to wrestle the book from her.

"No!" she shouted more loudly than she meant to.

She glanced at the chair where her cousin sat engrossed in a book of poetry, philosophy, or history.

"Very well, I shall not inquire about it, although I suspect Lady Catherine would not approve of your reading habits."

His smirk stirred Anne's doubt.

This was precisely the situation Mr. Wickham relished: a young lady taught to guard her virtue was sequestered virtually alone, without strict supervision. So it was this morning. Her governess, Miss Waygood, had gone on an errand, while her mother, Lady Catherine de Bourgh, visited with her sister, Lady Anne Darcy, in the drawing room down the hall. Only Fitzwilliam's presence afforded some safety.

"There is no call for suspicion," Wickham told her. "I think only of diverting you. Besides, what else will amuse you in this dreary library? Fitz is a dull lad, being on his best behavior today."

The two of them looked to where the only other occupant of the library sat quietly, giving every appearance of ignoring his companions.

Feeling confident of some privacy, Mr. Wickham settled against the desk and leaned forward to block Fitzwilliam's view. As he reached into his coat pocket and extracted several cards, a voice intoned from across the room, "She is not your cousin, Wickham."

Mr. Wickham rolled his eyes.

Anne stifled a laugh, for although Fitzwilliam's statement was true, there was no need to make a point of it. Gracious heaven, he was peevish this morning. His doltish comment only provoked her sympathy for George Wickham, who was her uncle Darcy's godson and namesake.

To her way of thinking, Mr. Wickham had sufficient reason to call her "cousin," for he and Fitzwilliam had been raised almost as brothers. Indeed, the two of them often quarreled like siblings, being unlike in temper and character. A particular bone of contention was their dissimilarity in fortune: whereas Fitzwilliam was the only son and heir to his father's Pemberley estates, Mr. Wickham was the son of Pemberley's former steward and must live on his godfather's largess.

Long inured to his rival's disdain, Wickham perceived no threat from that quarter and proceeded as planned.

He laid a card on the table.

Anne bent to examine it. The satirical print was of the type sold for two or three shillings in most print-shops. Fashionable London was much taken with graphic depictions of everyday life, especially those that mocked the Prince of Wales or ridiculed the elite caught by scandal. Any topic was cause for lampooning: marriage, adultery, cruelty and vice, beauty and frivolity, fashion, manners, politicians, body noises, animal passions of every pattern.

This print depicted a street scene in London's St. Giles's parish. Two scruffy boys threw dice on the cobblestones and ignored the grubby pickpocket stealing a gentleman's handkerchief; the dandy himself spoke to a pretty but dazed woman who had fallen down drunk. Near the water pump a lad of five or six appeared to be—what? making water? in the middle of a busy square? Surely not, Anne said to herself, although his stance looked suspicious.

"Do you find it interesting?"

"All things related to London are interesting," Anne replied. The less said about the print's details, the better, for no advantage accrued by encouraging him.

Mr. Wickham dealt three more cards, giving her time to review each one. The first two were pleasant street scenes of Cambridge and Yarmouth, while the last was rather vulgar, showing a raucous battle in which several constables wielded cudgels to break up a cock and hen club. In the excitement two bare-breasted women fought the crush.

The print's crudeness fascinated Anne, for she knew little of such characters in real life. She had never attended a club with rowdy friends, never conversed with gay women, never drunk spirits, never practiced seduction—such experiences were as foreign to her as those of the Hindu women in India. No doubt Mr. Wickham enjoyed these licentious behaviors and more.

Her temper jumped at his impudence. Why did he delight in tormenting her? Why did he resort to teasing when a little honey might advance her affection? His thinking was as impenetrable as a thickset holly hedge.

Mr. Wickham laid another card on the table. Titled "An EVENING'S INVITATION; with a WINK from the BAGNIO," it showed two well-dressed and bewigged harlots inviting a gentleman to sample their wares.

"Are you amused, cousin?"

Anne had no wish to answer the question, for she should not be asking herself daring questions as she looked into her tormentor's laughing eyes. How would it feel to be so intimate with Mr. Wickham that he would welcome, even encourage, my sliding a hand inside his shirt? Would I possess the nerve to do so? Would his skin be as soft and smooth as my own?

Fearing he might perceive her private thoughts, she regained her composure by asking a question. "What are these black spots on the women's faces? I have never seen anything like them. They appear in such odd places."

"They are beauty marks of a sort. Nothing that need concern you."

More than this Wickham would not say, for she was so naive, so much the country bumpkin, as to be unaware that artists painted black patches on their characters' faces as emblems of *alamode* disease, the much loathed but common venereal blight. "Do you admire the ladies' gowns?"

"Not in the least. They have been out of fashion for many years, and 'ladies' is a generous description, is it not? I thank you for the opportunity to view the prints, but they do not suit my taste."

"What of this one?" Wickham set a final card in front of her.

"Oh!" gasped Anne as she pushed to her feet. "You—you goat!" She had never imagined such behavior. Oh, she had seen the stallion mating with the mare and the bull with the cow. One could not live in the country without acquiring some knowledge of the natural order, but this … this depravity disgusted her.

"Does it offend you?"

"*You* offend me."

"No surprise there. I was sure the print would excite you. I have other equally thrilling views, if you are interested," he murmured, slipping an arm around her waist.

"No! Now leave me be. I was perfectly content until you interrupted my study."

"Not *perfectly* content, surely." He pressed his fingers against her spine. His free hand brushed her breast.

Anne pushed against his chest. Oh, the man was impossible. She was smiling up at him when she heard her name called.

"Anne, what goes on here?" bellowed Lady Catherine from the library doorway, her expression one of horror and disbelief. Uncle Darcy, standing at her elbow, turned his scrutiny first on Mr. Wickham and then on his niece. Fitzwilliam came to his feet as if from a deep sleep, confusion running across his face.

For several seconds everyone looked to Anne for an explanation. Her face flushed red as a raspberry. Wickham, naturally, was unperturbed. He relaxed against the library table, not an ort of remorse in his bones for the trouble he provoked.

Anne smoothed her gown. She was not sure how much her mother had seen, but her uncle looked confounded. The best course was to master her voice. "Mr. Wickham and I were debating—"

"Pray excuse me, ma'am—sir—I am at fault," said Wickham, the very model of contrition. "I fell to teasing Miss de Bourgh, much as a brother might do. Being a proper young lady, she objected to being called a bumpkin. You must not blame her."

Anne marveled at how readily the lie sprang to his lips. She glanced at her mother. Lady Catherine, confused by his gallantry, planted herself like a rock in the doorway.

Anne knew that look. Prompt action was expected. "I am ready, Mama," she said, picking up the book she had been studying. She shelved it in its rightful place, neatly stacked the others, and crossed the library. Her heart stood in her throat. When she drew near her uncle she stopped, submitted to his penetrating eye, and curtsied, before preceding her mother down the stairs to their waiting carriage.

Chapter 2

Two Dangers

Anne braced herself against the cold as she and her mother took their leave. A footman handed her into the barouche, where she settled against the squabs, her thoughts returning to the unfortunate event in Uncle Darcy's library.

She feared two dangers. The lesser risk was that uncle Darcy knew which book she had been reading: William Hunter's *Anatomia Uteri Humani Gravidi Tabulis Illustrata*, a collection of anatomical drawings of pregnant women. She had discovered it by accident the previous spring, when last her parents had brought her to London, and later learned her uncle had acquired it by purchasing the library of a friend, a deceased physician-accoucheur—the very same doctor whose collection included the censured great work of Aristotle.

On first glimpsing Dr. Hunter's engravings of the unborn child within its mother's womb, she had been appalled, almost sickened. One plate was shockingly real and repugnant: the mother's belly muscles and fat had been peeled back to reveal the cocooned child. The poor woman's butchered thighs were mere stumps, her legs having been sawed straight through like a carved pig. Their blunt ends seemed to glisten with bone and sinew and meat.

Anne had nearly gagged on beholding this rude violation, but after a few minutes she became enthralled by the soft fetal folds of flesh and the crush of the child's head as it pressed against the birth passage. How this exquisitely formed being grew in its mother's womb was a wonder. How the fully developed child could be forced from its mother's body was a near miraculous event. Having long hidden a fascination with the birth process in farm animals, her initial revulsion yielded to awe, fueling a peculiar drive to understand the anatomy detailed in Dr. Hunter's engravings.

Even if her uncle knew of her interest, she thought it unlikely that he would interfere, especially as he nearly always bowed to Sir Lewis's authority in raising his daughter. Everybody knew Sir Lewis de Bourgh was a liberal thinker.

The second danger and her deeper fear was Mr. Wickham's becoming aware of her inclination, for he might use his discovery against her in some unexpected way.

While these thoughts bounced around in Anne's head, Lady Catherine stepped up into the barouche and sat on the bench opposite. "Foolish girl. I am ashamed of you." The corners of her mouth pulled into a long frown as she turned a scornful eye on her daughter. "Such mortification you have caused. It will be some time before I hold my head high in your uncle's house." With this last pronouncement she pulled the check-string.

"Hie-yap" came the muffled command as Dawson jigged the reins and set the horses in motion.

The carriage jerked away from the curb.

Anne considered a soothing reply but found no words with which to defend herself. Try as she would to do right, her very person seemed to attract her mother's disfavor. Today she had been in trouble twice—not a record as offenses go but worrisome none the less, for her mother would extract a penance, the form of which could not be predicted.

She risked a glance at her mother. Lady Catherine was often intimidating, being a tall, large woman with strongly marked features, which might once have been handsome. Her manners expressed disdain for conduct less than perfectly correct, whether in company or among family. To Anne's frequent annoyance, her mother was inclined to enlighten the ignorant whenever the occasion presented itself, which was fairly often, there being no shortage of misbehaving servants, shopkeepers, clerics, children, squires, and even earls. For Mama, the entire world lay waiting for her instruction. At the moment her look bespoke a lecture.

"George Wickham of all people! What were you thinking to allow him to become so familiar with you, and in Fitzwilliam's presence? Mr. Wickham is nothing more than the son of a common steward and not worthy of your notice, much less your encouragement. True, none of us understand why your uncle continues to support him, but so it is."

While Lady Catherine pressed ahead with her scolding, Anne feigned a humble demeanor. She knew better than to glance out the carriage window, where London's street sellers hawked their flowers and fish; where coachmen yelled and cursed as they pushed their wagons, carts, and carriages through the tangled mass; where the neighs of a hundred horses and donkeys mingled with the shouts of sweeps clearing dung. To be animated by London's streets, to wish to throw oneself into the tangle of people thronging the side-walks and squares, to express any feeling other than contrition was to invite more criticism, and so she composed herself and considered the day's events.

Surely her behavior had not been so very bad. The morning's incident had been nothing more than giggles shared with

Dobbie, her maid, who described with great jocularity her nephew's impression of London on his first visit. "He went on and on about bear baitin' and cock throwin' and goose pullin', sayin' he'd never—"

"Goose pulling?" interrupted Anne.

"Aye, he made it sound a right form of recreation," said Dobbie, the very idea precipitating some glee between them as to how it might be done.

Their silliness had been ill-timed, for Lady Catherine had entered Anne's bedchamber just then, her eyebrows raised like flags on hearing giddy laughter during the normally solemn protocol of dressing. Later, in the morning room, Lady Catherine reminded Anne that it was not appropriate to befriend servants; a proud reserve would command her maid's respect and obedience.

The library affair was altogether different and carried some danger, but not for the reason her mother supposed. Anne's choice of reading material was far more likely to draw a violent reaction than Mr. Wickham's love-making.

For her to know or speak the words of the pregnant woman's anatomy—*uterus, placenta, fetus, funis*—was an offense against the gentler sensibility of women and, indeed, of all polite society. Her mother might never forgive her for such bold behavior.

"The time has come to secure a new governess for you," declared Lady Catherine, "as Miss Waygood cannot curb your animal impulses."

"Please, no, Mama! Miss Waygood is a dear companion, and I am learning much from her."

"You are not learning nearly enough if you believe such behavior as was displayed in the library is appropriate for a girl long out of the schoolroom and old enough to marry. What must your uncle think of you? He was surely as stunned as I to see you prancing about with his godson. He cannot approve such familiarity. Indeed, we all felt the keenest embarrassment."

"Mama, Miss Waygood wished to leave my uncle's house to visit a sister living in Cheapside. I had no reason to deny her such pleasure. And Mr. Wickham—"

"Do not present excuses," snapped Lady Catherine. "It does you no credit."

Anne turned to stare out the carriage window, where the sounds, sights, and smells of the Great Metropolis were now diminished. The rebuke ended; the penance claimed. She would lose her governess, her teacher, her confidant, her friend.

Lady Catherine observed the high color on Anne's cheeks. "We are nearly arrived at Chidham. You may use the time to think on your conduct and your father's probable view of it."

Her ladyship's eyes bored straight ahead. Her thin lips pressed into a frown of disapproval.

For Anne, her mother's frigid stare was as much a punishment as any hateful words. A heartfelt objection died on her tongue.

There was no arguing with Lady Catherine.

Chapter 3

The True Beauty

Chidham House was the de Bourgh family's London residence. Built when Anne was an infant and named after her paternal grandmother's family, the townhouse enjoyed an eastern aspect in Bedford Square.

From her third-floor window Anne observed the activity around the square in the morning gloom.

A red-faced drayman rubbed his hands together for warmth against the winter chill before seizing the reins and calling to his horses. On the south side a hired carriage rolled to a stop in front of General Hallett's house and waited while a man wearing a capacious greatcoat and gripping a black bag descended the steps; he tipped his hat to someone standing in the shadow of the doorway behind him and disappeared into the carriage. Perhaps a doctor had been called to attend General Hallett's mother, an elderly white-haired lady rarely seen in public these days, so Anne had heard. On the side-walk closer to home, two burly men balanced between them a large basket laden with root vegetables. They might be headed for the Chidham House kitchen.

Dobbie moved about the bedchamber, arranging her mistress's chemise, stockings, and morning gown.

There was no giggling.

"Come away from the window, Miss Anne, and let me dress you," said Dobbie. "Are you feelin' well? You are pale."

"I feel tolerably well," reassured Anne. No more was said while Dobbie helped her dress, for Anne had no heart for speaking of her governess's dismissal.

"Will you go down to breakfast?"

Anne slipped on her shoes and stood to examine her appearance in the looking-glass. Every aspect must be perfect if she hoped to escape her mother's criticism. "I shall go down now."

"You must be excited by the prospect of the Darcys coming here for tea on Thursday, and next week I hear there is to be a card party at Lord Matlock's. You are quite the Town lady!"

"I suppose."

Anne was distracted with imaginings of how she might prevent her mother from releasing Miss Waygood. Could she muster the resolve to challenge her mother's decision? Would doing so merely excite further censure? The prospect was daunting, for experience had taught her that such tactics seldom succeeded. She left Dobbie sorting her discarded night-clothes.

Lady Catherine was not in the dining room, which suited Anne well, for she feared another scolding. Skirting the table, she passed the servant who stood ready to serve and moved to examine the rolls, buns, and pound cake laid out on the sideboard. She had little appetite and so chose a plain roll and jam. The servant poured her a cup of tea. Anne sipped the scalding brew, nibbled on her roll, and recalled Mr. Wickham's trick in the library.

He delighted in vexing her. She found herself asking the same questions whenever they were in company together: Is his teasing an expression of his regard for me? Or is the opposite true—he torments me because he has no particular regard? Although he was a puzzle she could not solve, she had felt a thrill in his presence. The mere memory of his fingers brushing her breast made her heart leap. Those dark eyes, that sly grin—he was a dangerously attractive man.

"Miss Anne," called the butler from the doorway, interrupting her reverie. "Sir Lewis wishes to see you in the library."

Juggins was a rather crusty man who had served the de Bourgh family for nearly a decade. This morning he gave her a kindly look.

Anne forced a brave smile. "Thank you. I shall go now."

She walked with trepidation toward the back of the house where Sir Lewis's library was situated. Any other day she would relish time spent with her dear Papa in his private retreat. So long as she promised to be quiet, he allowed her to claim a padded chair near the fire, where she might read or draw and rest her feet on an embroidered stool.

Sometimes he asked her to fetch a book, which she did quick as lightning, for she knew the location of every item on the library's many shelves. Sometimes he would call to her: "What say you about the benefits of mixing wine with the ground corns and parings of a horse's foot as a cure for cancer? It seems a waste of good wine to me." Or: "I see the Royal Jennerian Society is busy writing letters to *The Gentleman's Magazine*. The Society is not yet a year old and must clarify for a confused public the principles for discerning the cow-pox from the small-pox." Or: "Listen to this remarkable poem titled 'Bonaparte's Soliloquy' …" On rare occasions, he would open a book or magazine, saying, "Look at this—" At his invitation, she laid down her pencils and stood at his elbow to learn the topic of his study, which might be a drawing of a country church or a stone castle or a silver artifact dug out of a slate quarry. While he shared his opinion, she watched his long fingers tap a page or trace a cathedral arch. She heard the affection in his voice. Today, however, her stomach fluttered as she knocked on the thick oaken door.

"Come."

"Did you wish to speak with me, Papa?"

"Yes. Sit here, love," he replied, pointing to a chair positioned next to his desk. "Don't look so morose! I shall not heckle you." When she settled into the chair, he said, "I must ask a question. What did Mr. Wickham say to you in your uncle's library?"

"He merely teased me about being dull and reading too many books. You know his nature. He is easily bored and could not resist pestering me for being studious."

Sir Lewis waited.

A dog's bark was heard in the square. A faggot laid atop the grate's glowing coals popped, sending sparks up the chimney.

"According to your mother, Mr. Wickham appeared overly friendly. It would not surprise me to hear of it, for he seems bent on ignoring propriety. Did he say or do anything improper?"

Anne felt confident his version of the event was nothing like the one her mother had relayed to him.

"He showed me several popular prints, including one of Cambridge and another of Yarmouth's main street. It is a mystery why he thought Yarmouth might interest me, although the drawing was prettily done, especially as it showed a regiment of soldiers." Her tongue wanted to run on, which might cause trouble.

"That is all? He did nothing unseemly?"

Anne shook her head and struggled to keep her expression neutral.

Sir Lewis's brow wrinkled as if he suspected she hid some egregious tale, but his features softened when he spoke. "Remember what Pamela's parents wrote in a letter when they were concerned about her safety: 'It is virtue and goodness only, that make the true beauty.' You must always be thinking of how to preserve your honor. You are a sensible girl, Anne. I am sure you will learn not to be persuaded by charm and good looks."

How very like her father to cite Richardson's novel. In *Pamela* he would have seen a story of manners and characters that might instruct her, unlike her mother, who perceived only a theatrical, overwrought novel of little use to anyone except the publisher.

How Papa could have troubled himself to read it was a mystery, for privately, she and her dearest friend, Tilly Sullen, agreed with Mama for once. Pamela was stupid to allow herself to be maneuvered into compromising situations with the son of her deceased employer and silly to marry him. Pamela's grumbling and wailing, her fits and fainting, her laments over threats to her virtue, and her lack of imagination for escaping the clutches of the vile, horse-lipped Mrs. Jewkes, all pointed to a weak, sniveling character.

In truth, *Shamela*, being wonderfully facetious, was more to their liking.

Had Papa read all her favorite novels? *Evelina*? *Cecilia*? Did he know she and Tilly read gothic novels: *The Castle of Wolfenbach*, *The Mysteries of Udolpho*, *The Monk*, *The Midnight Bell*? Had he been as thoroughly scared and bewildered by *The Necromancer* as they? Probably not, but he was a remarkable man to allow her the liberty of reading whatever was of interest to her. Did Mama task him for it?

"Where Mr. Wickham is concerned," Sir Lewis continued, "I charge you to be on your guard. He lacks Fitzwilliam's good manners and common sense."

"Yes, Papa." She twisted her fingers together, trying to work up the courage to speak her mind. "Papa, I fear Mama intends to find a new governess for me. Will you intervene on my behalf? Please. I could have no better or dearer friend than Miss Waygood. She is like a sister to me."

Sir Lewis returned a gentle smile.

"You know I never interfere with Lady Catherine's plan for turning my unruly daughter into a lady. Now, you must get dressed for a walk. I hear Miss Waygood has a treat for you."

Chapter 4

Some Souls Speak

"I saw the sweetest hat at Miss Thornbury's shop. It will suit you very well," said Miss Waygood as she pulled on her gloves and swept a sharp eye over her charge. "I believe you need fresh air, for you look pale and disagreeable. Shall we go?"

Anne followed her governess out into the square, from which they set off at a brisk pace. "Isabelle, slow down! I'm half out of breath."

"I can see that. Have you not been sleeping well? Perhaps London's many charms are keeping you awake at night. I hope that is not the case, for I hear you have a busy calendar."

Isabelle linked her arm with Anne's. Their easy gait assured any passerby of their companionship. Indeed, they might have been thought sisters, with Miss Waygood being the elder, her counting four and twenty years since her birthday to Anne's seventeen. Their coloring differed, however. Where Miss Waygood's perfectly oval face drew admiration for its dark eyes framed by rich brown curls, Anne's plainer visage was marked by hazel eyes set beneath straight hair the color of damp mushrooms; and their figures were most dissimilar, with Miss

Waygood tending toward a stout but becoming plumpness, while Anne was petite and girlish.

Indeed, most everyone would admit Miss Waygood was pretty, but not beautiful in the classical style. In profile her face presented a smallish nose, full lips, and a strong chin.

"Miss Waygood leads with her bosom and expects the rest of her body to keep pace," observed Tilly one morning as the two friends watched the governess storm across Hunsford's green, her pelisse flapping behind her.

Anne knew the truth of this, for Miss Waygood seldom glided; she flew before the wind, whether traversing the great hall or striding the garden paths of Rosings Park. Such quickness was surprising in a lady with such a full figure, but fortunately her hurried movements were pleasing rather than comical.

"I sleep very well," Anne replied, "and find London exciting."

"Yes, the Great Metropolis weaves its spell and after a day or two we forget ourselves, become frivolous and gay, and lose our moral compass." This last was said with some vehemence. "Did Sir Lewis speak with you about Mr. Wickham? I understand there was a disturbance in Mr. Darcy's library yesterday. You must know Mr. Wickham is a troublemaker of the first water. He will not do for you, so don't encourage him."

Anne was growing tired of being told what she could and could not do.

"He likes to act a devil," she said, "and Mama reminds me often enough of his low birth, but I don't understand why everybody is so against him. *Why* is he not worthy? My uncle seems to think of him as one of his family, for he includes Mr. Wickham in most family gatherings at Pemberley and here in Town. I heard Mama say Mr. Wickham shall join Fitzwilliam at Cambridge. Surely my uncle would not send him to university if he did not believe him to be intelligent and capable."

"Mr. Darcy likely expects Mr. Wickham to enter the Church, which is why he will receive an education." Miss Waygood pulled Anne to one side to let a bonny lady with four rowdy children in tow pass on the side-walk.

"That is why this is all so puzzling," said Anne. "Mr. Wickham's attending Cambridge alongside Fitzwilliam will only enhance his status. At university he will meet and befriend the sons of the aristocracy, and if he later enters the Church, he will be considered respectable, despite his humble birth. Many a vicar or rector has married the daughter of a gentleman or baronet or even a peer. I cannot understand why he has such a sad reputation. He isn't bookish like Fitzwilliam, true, but he has pleasing manners and a lively spirit."

More than this she would not say, for she found Mr. Wickham exceptionally attractive: his clothing fit his tall, lithe frame well; his brown eyes shone beneath a noble brow; and his disposition, which could sometimes be overly mischievous, was mostly agreeable.

He had all the best part of beauty, which was why she had trouble resisting his charm.

"Besides, I have known him all my life," she told Isabelle, "and although his tricks and schemes are often maddening, I will say this: he appears interested in my person, unlike Fitzwilliam, who rarely condescends to speak to me."

"Anne! You are sadly lacking in character if you cannot appreciate your cousin's superiority to Mr. Wickham. Mr. Darcy is a descendant of the first Earl of Matlock, just as you are, and he is a gentleman in the truest sense of the word. He is at all times sensible of other people's feelings. He is kind and thoughtful. He is a man of intelligence and integrity. I think it likely the two of you are expected to marry one day—an event about which we have speculated numerous times during our acquaintance—and if our surmise proves correct, then you will be treated with respect and enjoy every consideration as Mr. Darcy's wife."

"Every consideration except affection!" Anne barked. "Is there any affection in this case? I know little of these matters, having never been allowed to become acquainted with any man who might capture my fancy, but in my view Fitzwilliam is about as inviting as a cold eel pie—so forbidding in his manner and countenance, so—"

Miss Waygood laughed. "You have been reading too many romantic novels."

"Perhaps, but Mr. Wickham, at least—"

"Do not fall under Mr. Wickham's spell. Sir Lewis and Lady Catherine will never permit you to marry him."

Anne could picture her mother flaying Mr. Wickham alive if he should mention marriage, for she feared Lady Catherine expected her to marry Fitzwilliam.

Nothing had been said to her directly, but she suspected her mother and aunt agreed on the idea. The sisters imagined enlarging the family's wealth and status by wedding their family estates—the Darcy's Pemberley estates in Derbyshire and the de Bourgh's estate, Rosings Park, near Hunsford in Kent—and thereby increasing the family's land ownership. Such was the plan, no doubt, but had the conspirators considered whether their children might grow to resent the obligation?

On her side, Anne could not imagine marrying Fitzwilliam. They seemed always to rub against each other, and her heart rebelled at the idea of being forced to act on duty alone.

Why could she not marry for affection? And what were Fitzwilliam's thoughts on the matter? He had not spoken to her of their prospective marriage, if such was the case, which struck her as unusual, his being older and a man, which gave him more authority. Surely his own view warranted expression, if only to reassure her of his warm regard.

Of course, he might not know of the engagement plan, but as things stood, his looks and manner did not suggest any tender feelings on his side. Although she had never felt the force of a man's affection—she sometimes thought Mr. Wickham's ogling was mostly designed to torment, not attach—she knew a warm look when she saw it.

"What you say is true, but Fitzwilliam never looks at me the way Mr. Dighurst looks at you."

Miss Waygood came to a full stop and gripped Anne's arm, oblivious to passing pedestrians.

"Do not speak so," she warned in a low voice. "I will not have it put about that Mr. Dighurst has any design on me. Do you understand?" Anne nodded mutely. "Good. We are almost arrived at the milliner's shop, where we shall have more pleasant matters to entertain us."

Anne shrank at Isabelle's sudden distemper.

Mr. Dighurst was the only son of Major and Mrs. Dighurst, a happy couple who leased Bardolph Hall, a smallish manor situated near the village of Hunsford and not far from Rosings. Mr. Dighurst's regard for Miss Waygood could be perceived by anybody with a pair of working eyes, and right from their first being introduced. Of course, Miss Waygood took care to show him no more consideration than she showed any other man, for she could not risk ruining her reputation in the neighborhood or embarrassing her employer. But Anne, who knew her better than anybody, had detected an early attraction and observed its progression to a deeper affection over the course of the past year. The couple were discreet, but their regard for each other could not be hidden. If Anne saw their souls speak, was it not possible that other observers did as well?

Chapter 5

Marching Orders

Darcy House was situated on the north side of Charles Street, only a stone's throw from Berkeley Square and close to Lansdowne House, which anchored the east end of the street. The location had been chosen for its quiet aspect and respectable residents. The Darcys preferred this comfortable side street to the bustle of a large Town square, which decision Lady Anne Darcy found herself defending whenever her sister called.

"There is such a jumble of carriages and carts around Lansdowne House this morning," complained Lady Catherine as she swept into the drawing room and took a sofa. While she arranged her shawl she gave Anne a quick nod to indicate where she should sit. "I do not know how you tolerate the crowd in this area. One would think Mr. Pitt still leased the house, which he very well may be doing. He's maneuvering for another premiership, no doubt."

"We've seen his carriage passing in the street, of course," Lady Anne replied, refusing to be nettled by a discussion of traffic or Pitt's political ambitions or, indeed, by anything her sister might say. "You will never guess who called on me yesterday: Lady Anne Barnard, whom we met before she traveled with her husband to the Cape of Good Hope. She told me several amusing stories about her life there. Two years ago, in February, she said the temperature in Cape Town reached one hundred and four degrees in the shade. Can you imagine it?"

"I have no wish to imagine it and, indeed, hardly remember the lady," Lady Catherine replied with her usual frankness. "Why any woman would follow her husband to such a wild and ungovernable outpost is a mystery. Presumably her reward for such long suffering is the privilege of returning to our superior British soil. Does Mrs. Thornsby still reside in Berkeley Square?"

"Yes, oh, yes, she has—"

"Her townhouse stands near that of Lady Sarah Fane, I believe. Have you heard the rumor? Lady Sarah shall marry Lord Villiers next year. Two great families to be united! Only think of the settlements to be drawn up. Their wedding will be the talk of the Town."

While the sisters dissected the family trees of the Earls of Westmorland and Jersey, Anne busied herself imagining her wedding to Mr. Wickham. Mellow light spilled through stained glass windows and enshrouded them in a warm glow. Papa stood on one side, her lover on the other. Dressed in a white embroidered gown, her head crowned with a sweet bonnet festooned with rose buds, she looked an angel: graceful, ethereal, loving. Mr. Wickham, virile and confident, dazzled in his silk suit. His eyes spoke truly; he worshiped her. The ceremonial words infused them with the scents of love and contentment and perfection. Only their vessels of desire remained to be filled.

"Your aunt and I wish to share some news with you," said Lady Catherine. "Anne!"

Anne awoke to her mother's sharp entreaty.

"I wish you to pay attention. When you were an infant many years ago, we—by which I mean your aunt and uncle Darcy, along with your father and myself—agreed that you and Fitzwilliam shall marry. We waited to speak of it until you were sufficiently mature to appreciate our plan. From this day you may enjoy the benefit of receiving your family's blessing and know your future is secure."

Her ladyship's smile was beatific, almost superior, as if the angel Gabriel himself had informed her personally of the happy event.

Not expecting such an important proclamation to follow on the heels of idle chat about two earls she had never met, Anne blurted, "I don't want to marry Fitzwilliam." The words were cast before she had taken a moment to think. A ruddy quake crossed Lady Catherine's face, causing Anne to add, "I mean no insult to my dear aunt and uncle or, indeed, to you and Papa. Fitzwilliam is a man of intelligence and dignity"—she smiled at aunt Darcy, sitting so still on the sofa opposite that she seemed to be holding her breath—"but I am convinced we would not suit."

Into a deepening silence she felt compelled to add: "I believe our characters are too dissimilar to produce felicity in marriage, and …"—she began to lose confidence, her voice dropping to a whisper—"and I prefer to choose my husband."

Lady Catherine looked apoplectic.

Anne shrank under her mother's glare.

The housemaids setting teacups and cakes on the sideboard paused.

"Your preference is of no consequence to me." Lady Catherine's spine stiffened. "A decision has been made. You are merely being informed of it. I am sorry to realize that I was mistaken in you, for you seem not to understand that considerable thought has been given to your marriage, not only by your parents but by your larger family, including your grandparents. Lord and Lady Matlock likewise approve of the match. Your marrying Fitzwilliam will increase our status and consequence in society and produce an heir who will inherit your father's baronetcy. Indeed, one day I expect to see Fitzwilliam elevated to the peerage, and that outcome depends upon your marriage."

Disapproval glowed in her eyes. "You must realize my marriage to Sir Lewis was arranged by my parents, as is commonly done among families of our rank. We were introduced, met two or three times during the negotiations, and have made a success of it. Our characters and wishes never entered into the decision, for we both knew our duty. I had thought you understood yours."

Feeling the force of her mother's resentment, Anne glanced at her aunt, seeking she knew not what. Support? Permission to disagree with the decision?

Aunt Darcy's expression was unreadable.

"Nothing else remains to be said on the matter," Lady Catherine informed her, "although I shall apprise Sir Lewis of your willful opinion. He will be displeased to learn that you expressed your views so freely. I suggest you remove yourself to some quiet place—the library might suit—where you can contemplate your disobedience."

Turning to her sister, Lady Catherine said, "Are the Alfriston-Seals in Town? I understood they might be expected this week."

Chapter 6

A Truth He Dare Not Speak

"Little fool!" muttered Fitzwilliam Darcy as he pushed open the heavy library door and nearly butted the butler. "Pardon me, Jacobs. I thought the room was empty."

"No matter, sir. I have checked the grate. Do you wish a fire laid?"

"If you would be so good."

Fitzwilliam moved to a bookcase and pretended to search for a book. Behind him, the butler fussed with matches and kindling, the job of lighting a fire in the library not being a duty that fell within his purview. As the faggots spluttered to life, Jacobs bowed his way into the hall, annoyed at being asked to perform so menial a duty, but wondering what had upset the young Master.

Alone at last, Fitzwilliam yanked a book from the shelf and strode to the window, where he surveyed the south side of Charles Street. A young man of consequence and good fortune, he was poised to turn twenty years of age in two months' time and claimed all the proper virtues, being tall, handsome, and manly. Intelligent, too, and so Mr. Ellis had reminded him a few weeks ago. "You have a newcomer's anxiety about beginning your studies at Cambridge," the tutor told him, "but your scholarly discipline will carry you over any rough patches. I harbor no fear that you shall fall prey to drunkenness and frivolity, for you hold dear the great university's motto: *hinc lucem et pocula sacra*—from here, light and sacred draughts," which Fitzwilliam knew referred to the university as a source of enlightenment and valuable knowledge.

His tutor, no less than his own dear father, had no doubt of his success at university or in life, for he had been taught the values of determination and duty from an early age. His manners were elegant; his character admirable, if a little reserved; and his preference always for a glimpse of the rustic vistas from the tall windows of his family's house in Derbyshire.

London made him peevish.

The endless round of social calls, however much deemed necessary, depressed his spirit. He would sooner be riding across the home fields or discussing animal stock with his father's steward in Pemberley's stable yard. On the best of days London's grit and chaos, its mean streets and vile smells, its encroaching young ladies (bent on catching his eye) wore him down, and now his cousin acted like a spoiled child, spouting her opinions for all and sundry.

He reminded himself to breathe, to release the anger that bound his heart on overhearing Anne protest her engagement: "I don't want to marry Fitzwilliam."

He had been approaching the front drawing room with the idea of greeting his aunt and cousin when he overheard Anne's remark. Of all the thoughtless, rude comments to make, with servants setting the tea table and a footman in the hall. What humiliation. Her declaration will be the topic *du jour* over dinner in the kitchen and out in the mews. The girl is silly and bird-witted and I don't want to marry her either.

This thought, rising like bile, made him pause, for it was a truth he dare not speak. He had known of their engagement for several years. When the case was explained to him, he challenged his father: "Why must I be nice to her? She's boring and a girl."

His open denunciation of his intended's charms brought a gentle rebuke. "She will one day be your wife," his father had said, "and it is better to learn a little of her character and habits now than to find yourself ignorant of them on your wedding day."

Fitzwilliam accepted this advice in the same spirit as he received the order to study literature, mathematics, Greek, and Latin. It was his duty—a somewhat nebulous concept to his tender twelve-year-old mind—and since his beloved father expected him to apply himself, it must be a worthy endeavor. But as the years passed, he began to chafe at the idea. He had seen enough of the world to state his ideal: a pretty, vivacious woman with talent and intelligence and a warm heart. A dark-haired, long-legged beauty with a womanly form would suit very well. Anne was the opposite of everything desirable in a woman. She was timid in company, thin and plain and ordinary in appearance, and sometimes boyish in manner. He did not care to know her, much less marry her, and therein lay the problem: his excellent parents, whom he loved and felt honor-bound to obey, expected him to do his duty.

How shocked they would be to behold his true heart, which sometimes fell prey to sparkling laughter and a handsome figure. Why could he not accept his duty to marry Anne? What did it say of his character that he allowed himself to be attracted to other women? Could he force himself to yield to a duty he found repugnant?

So black was his heart that he could not speak of his feelings even to Mr. Curlew, a dear friend and former vicar, now retired, who lived near Pemberley. He could imagine the elderly Mr. Curlew telling him what he did not want to hear, his gravelly voice echoing Moses on the Mount. "You serve God by honoring your parents' wishes, my son, and remember what Seneca wrote: nothing deters a good man from doing what is honorable." Mr. Curlew had no need to remind him that the Holy Scripture espoused ten commandments, of which two were particularly troubling: "honor thy father and thy mother" and "thou shalt not covet."

The biblical list did not begin to cover his sins. Thou shalt not desire a different wife from the one chosen for you. Thou shalt not feel aroused by a pair of fine eyes, a rosebud mouth, or a graceful form. Thou shalt not dislike your cousin.

He heard the library door open. Anne stood on the threshold, her eyes ablaze, defiance stamped on her features. Not caring to speak to her, he took his favorite chair facing the windows and opened his book.

At this display of haughtiness, the young lady marched forward, her head held high. She strode across the carpeted floor to the far end of the room, where she pulled an overlarge book from a low shelf, laid the heavy tome on a table with a thump, and sat down to study.

Tension rode the room for many minutes, with only the occasional crinkly turn of a bound page or the fall of a sooty faggot disturbing the peace. Gloomy shadows fell across the room, bringing a chill, until a housemaid arrived to light the girandole candles.

Anne could not concentrate.

Her eyes were drawn to the back of Fitzwilliam's head. She wondered whether he had only today learned of their engagement and, like her, resented the idea, felt powerless to fight it, and so retreated to this quiet sanctum to think. The flash in his eyes told her much. Had they shared a true affection, they might unite in their dislike of the plan and work to overthrow it, but she knew not how to achieve such accord.

He probably thought she had not anticipated this day or understood her mother's hundred hints. He probably believed she supported their mothers' wishes. She tried bringing her attention back to her opened book, but her mind soon returned to the drawing room scene. How strange that she and Fitzwilliam had not been brought together to hear the news. Equally odd was her aunt's demeanor. Aunt Darcy had neither defended nor condemned the decision, suggesting an unease about the telling, which Anne thought might be wishful thinking on her part.

Anne startled when Fitzwilliam stood to stir the fire. Perhaps he felt her scrutiny. When he sat down again she took up her thoughts.

What traits could she and her cousin claim in common? His life was not much different from hers. He was his family's heir and thus treated with respect, if not always with affection, by the staff and tenants and village folk. He walked the Darcy properties with his father, he guided and supported the Darcy tenants, he knew all the Darcy servants. She did much the same at Rosings. They had their status as heirs and their family connections in common.

It was their characters that differed. No! That's not quite right, she said to herself. We both adore our fathers. We both love our homeland and want to do right by our servants and tenants. Long after our fathers are gone, we hope one day to know, deep in our bones, that they would have approved our good and honest actions. Neither of us would consciously dishonor our fathers. Neither of us would risk harming our estates or their peoples.

In these ways our characters are alike, but we differ in other ways. Fitzwilliam seeks a pretty lady who will bring vivacity and warmth to his hearth—a woman to make him proud. The problem is that I will never be a beauty or even handsome. I care little for status and social position, however so much I am told I should do so. My heart cannot be won with fine gifts and elegant manners. I wish to choose my husband, to marry for love, to have a chance for true happiness. Fitzwilliam is an attractive man, that I can allow, but he is driven by pride. He is proud of his good looks, proud of his intelligence, proud of the Darcy family and himself. With so much pride in his heart, there can be no room for passion.

This thought steered her mind in a new direction. Try as she would, she could not picture her cousin's love-making: the shy smile, the stolen kiss, a tender look.

When the library door opened, Anne turned at the sound. A plump, rosy-cheeked housemaid approached. "Lady Catherine asked me to fetch you. The carriage stands out front."

"Tell her I shall come directly."

Chapter 7

Plain Speaking

The short drive from the Darcy townhouse in Charles Street to Chidham House in Bedford Square seemed interminable. Anne glanced occasionally at her mother's rigid face but received no sign of recognition. The strident cries of street vendors and draymen masked the uneven thrum of the carriage wheels, but no comfort could be found watching London's fashionable couples strolling along the side-walk, apparently oblivious to the November damp. On arriving at Chidham House, Lady Catherine descended from the carriage and proceeded up the steps into the entrance hall without a backward glance.

Anne understood: she was pretty much done for.

"What's the matter, love?" asked Dobbie as her gnarled fingers worked to unbutton Anne's gown. "You look all done in. Have you received bad news?"

Tears welled up at the affection in her maid's voice. "Oh, Dobbie! I am in more trouble than a kettle of fish dangling over a fire. Mama is fit to strangle me. I expect you'll see a notice of my demise in the broadsides tomorrow after my body is found floating in the river." She wiped tears from her cheeks.

"You goose. You can have done nothin' so bad as to think your mother will murder you. Now, tell me what your trouble is, leavin' out all the hysterical bits."

Anne stopped fidgeting while Dobbie helped her put on a fresh gown. "Mama and my aunt told me that I am expected to marry Fitzwilliam." She stared at her maid, her eyes wide with astonishment and indignation. "Fitzwilliam!"

Dobbie's mind worked this over. "I am right pleased to hear it. Such a handsome young man is young Mr. Darcy." She checked the line of buttons and smoothed the gown's shoulders. "Your family has chosen a fine husband for you."

Anne fell across the bed. "You don't know the half of it, Dobbie."

"Please sit up, love, or your gown will be creased. Tell me which half I don't know, for I think it very good news."

"I told them I don't want to marry Fitzwilliam."

Dobbie chuckled to herself. "Now that is as tall a tale as you've ever told. You would never say such a thing, and why should you? Mr. Darcy is kind and smart and possesses every proper feeling."

"I speak the truth! I don't want to marry him."

A tentative knock was followed by the form of the youngest housemaid, Betsy. She curtsied. "Miss, Sir Lewis has asked to speak with you. He's in the library."

Anne shot Dobbie a forlorn look.

"I go to my doom," she said, rising to follow Betsy down the stairs. The library door stood cracked an inch or two. She inhaled deeply and beat a soft tattoo on the wooden panel. "Papa?"

"Come," came the curt answer.

Anne stepped into the room and approached her father, who sat rather rigidly, his elbows resting on the wooden arms of his old library chair; the tips of his long fingers, pressed together, formed a steeple over his lap. She forced herself to look him in the eye, where she caught a hard squint.

Sir Lewis waved an arm to indicate his wish that she stand on the opposite side of the desk.

"I have heard a report of you that I find hard to believe, and thus I ask you directly: Did you tell your mother and aunt that you have no wish to marry Fitzwilliam?"

"Yes, Papa."

After a long silence, Sir Lewis asked, "What is the basis for your objection to marrying him?"

Not having been expected to be asked such a question, Anne could think of no immediate answer.

Sir Lewis was prepared to wait.

"Fitzwilliam is kind and smart and possesses every proper feeling," Anne replied a little unsteadily, thinking there could be no harm in repeating Dobbie's comments.

After another long wait, Sir Lewis asked, "But you object to these virtues?"

"Oh, no! He is a very good sort of person, but I cannot talk to him." Determining, rightly, that her father would never accept so inadequate an answer, she added, "He is clever, but sometimes selfish and overbearing and nearly always superior in his thinking, by which I mean, he values his own opinion above all others and dislikes hearing any of my views. Indeed, I think it irritates him when I express my opinions or ideas, as though he believes I have no right to share them."

She began to give the question serious thought. Why did she dislike Fitzwilliam? Was it truly dislike or merely a lack of understanding? If she knew him better, would she find him more agreeable? "I don't think we have much in common. He is studious and loves reading Greek and Latin and poetry. I like drawing and music and novels and walking the fields with you." She was struck by a surprising insight. "Frankly, I'm not the sort of girl he finds attractive. I could better imagine marrying Richard."

Not until she expressed this opinion did she recognize the truth of it. Her cousin Richard Fitzwilliam, the younger son of her mother's brother, Lord Matlock, was an agreeable character with surprising wit. She was never troubled by his teasing and often tried to provoke it.

"That idea you can cast aside, for Matlock will never entertain it." Sir Lewis gazed across the desk, an inscrutable look on his face. "Let me speak plainly. First, we are all selfish, overbearing, and superior in our thinking, which makes your criticism of him unworthy, for you are as guilty of these faults as he. More to the point, your parents have given considerable thought to the issue of whom you should marry. Fitzwilliam has much to offer you personally, being both scholarly and worldly, besides being a man of good character and breeding. He has known of your engagement for several years, but Lady Catherine and I chose to delay telling you of it until you were somewhat older. You are nearly eighteen, Anne, and shall be presented at Court next spring. You are old enough to marry, and many a young lady of your age and situation has done so. What astonishes me is that you failed to understand or respect your parents' wishes."

While Sir Lewis gazed thoughtfully at his daughter, Anne's lower lip began to tremble. She stared down at his magnifying glass laid carelessly across an open book. When next he spoke, she compelled herself to look at him even though her eyes glistened with tears.

"Had we learned at any time that Fitzwilliam had a disreputable character or was mean-spirited, we would have withdrawn our agreement to your marriage, but that has not been the case. He is, by every standard, a decent and dignified fellow, and your mother and I are fond of him. We have never had the least qualm about his behavior or character and know that we can rely on him to do his duty. We expect the same of you."

"Yes, Papa."

"There remains but one action for you to perform before I can consider this issue understood on all sides."

"Yes, Papa. I shall apologize to my aunt and to Mama for my indiscretion."

"Good," he said as he picked up his magnifying glass. "Close the door behind you, please."

Anne dropped a small curtsy and complied. Her knees felt wobbly as she climbed the stairs.

Chapter 8

Misery and Man

Anne stuffed her cold hands inside her muff while she waited for Miss Waygood. A wasp's nest of worries plagued her as she stood staring down into the hearth's grate, where no fire had been lit. The apology to her mother had left her feeling as bruised as a trampled peach.

Lady Catherine's steely eyes reflected triumph as she sat regally at her desk in the morning room. "I had not thought you so spoiled as to be nearly beyond amendment," said her ladyship before next summarizing her daughter's many failings, lecturing about the duty owed her family, and complaining of the mortification she caused everybody, herself in particular.

Anne had stood as if summoned before an aggrieved and intolerant judge, her head bowed, her eyes honed on the tips of her slippers. She awaited sentencing in silence. Throughout her trial her demeanor was reserved and her tears genuine, which gave Lady Catherine some satisfaction. In fact, these tears had nothing to do with her mother's harsh words, which Anne hardly attended, but arose on recalling her father's displeasure. His censure was a heartache deeply felt. How might she regain his approval when she took no pleasure in her engagement? Should she speak to her cousin? Dare she hope they might together figure out how to change their fate? Could she change Miss Waygood's fate as well?

Her mother's parting words only served to heighten her fear: "Tell Miss Waygood I wish to speak with her, after which you may accompany her to your aunt's house."

"Yes, Mama," said Anne, her heart aching like a tender fester at her governess's probable reckoning. It seemed their sisterly affection would be destroyed and her future carved in stone. She would marry Fitzwilliam, as was expected, and Miss Waygood would leave the family's employ. Lady Catherine was not one to forget or rescind a decision.

Would that she could influence her mother and change the future. Anne pictured herself standing resolutely before Lady Catherine, her voice steady and forceful, her bearing proud, while she defended Miss Waygood in a rational and competent manner. Her brilliant arguments had the happy outcome of changing her mother's determined course. This imagining nearly made Anne smile, for the success of her make-believe effort was the first such instance and nothing like the rebuke she herself had endured.

"Humph," she snorted to the chilly shadows. You green-goose. Why do you torture yourself in this fashion? No good will come from these idle fancies, for you lack the power of persuasion. Until you gain this worthy art you cannot bend your mother's will.

"Come," called Miss Waygood from the doorway. "We must carry umbrellas, for it looks like rain."

No words were spoken as they walked along Oxford Street. Anne felt like she was taking a ride to Tyburn, the spot of the infamous tree at the corner of Hyde Park where for more than five hundred years felons had been hanged. Nobody had been executed on the gallows there in twenty years, but an image of the Tyburn tree stood firm in Anne's mind: it was as formidable and unbendable as her mother's will.

"Isabelle—" said Anne after they turned down Regent Street and headed toward Piccadilly.

"Shh," replied Miss Waygood on detecting anxiety in Anne's voice. "We will do everything as expected. Shall we stop at Fortnum and Mason? You mentioned wanting to browse there, and I might buy some tea."

Anne kept her composure as they entered the popular shop. Despite being crowded with shoppers seeking packets of spices and canisters of tea and coffee, it took only minutes to collect honey, dried fruit, and Scotch eggs for the house staff, which she directed to be delivered to Mrs. Dobbie at No. __ Bedford Square.

"Is your mother aware that you buy goods for the staff?" asked Miss Waygood. "Do they not also receive vails?"

"They do, but Papa gave me two pounds before we left Rosings, which allows me to be generous. They have little time to venture into this part of town, and Dobbie loves Scotch eggs." Anne scribbled a note and handed it to the clerk.

These sorts of transactions could be complicated, for she knew her mother would not approve of her generosity. Her father, on the other hand, permitted all indulgences—well, all indulgences except her wish not to marry her cousin. "Do we have other errands before calling on my aunt?" Her easy fellowship with Miss Waygood and the very ordinariness of these activities made her teary eyed. Soon, she feared, her governess would no longer accompany her on these outings. It was too much, this fear of losing her dear friend and confidant while also dreading an impending marriage to her cousin. Had she simply remained behind at Rosings and not traveled to London, none of these problems would exist. Her life would have gone on as before, free of aggravations and uncertainties. It was unfortunate that she had looked forward to this visit, for now the city was emptied of all its enchantments.

"Let's order tea," suggested Miss Waygood on perceiving Anne's distress. "Would you care to partake of refreshments at Gunter's, as we did last week? Berkeley Square isn't that far from here."

Anne shrugged one shoulder. What joy could ever be hers if Miss Waygood no longer resided at Rosings?

Miss Waygood took Anne's arm. "Now, Anne, a lady, regardless of age or position, must always know her own mind. It will not do to allow someone else to make an important decision for you. In fact, to make no decision is itself a kind of decision, if one thinks on the matter, and such aimlessness may have severe consequences if it gives the impression a lady is susceptible to influence." Miss Waygood steered her young charge along the side-walk. "What could be more important than choosing the best seat for enjoying a cup of tea?"

Anne could hardly bear to be teased by Miss Waygood, whose winning ways nearly always gladdened her heart. Today's gentle lecture about proper etiquette and the finer shades of feminine decorum smote her heart, for what was she doing in submitting to marriage but proving herself susceptible to her parents' influence? She had made a decision about her marriage to Fitzwilliam but could not act on it.

Shortly after they settled themselves and ordered their refreshments, Miss Waygood said, "I wish to speak of my meeting with your mother this morning."

"You will be leaving Rosings," stated Anne, her tone rather more matter-of-fact than her feelings implied.

"Yes. It is time I did so."

"Please don't leave me," pleaded Anne. "I cannot bear to be at Rosings without you."

This outburst surprised Miss Waygood and startled several patrons sitting nearby. One well-dressed matron scowled her contempt for Anne's unguarded emotion.

"You must realize I cannot live at Rosings forever, however pleasing its situation," Miss Waygood said, thinking Anne's resistance to the idea might be expected, since she was girlish in some ways and surprisingly mature in others.

"You know how Mama finds fault with me," Anne continued in a more reserved manner. "Your counsel checks my temper at Mama's interference. Your voice soothes me when I am brought to tears. Your face mirrors my ambitions, for you hold to teaching me more than the dance of the drawing room." Impulsively she reached across the table and grasped Miss Waygood's hand. "I thought you were happy at Rosings. I have believed us to be good friends. Surely you cannot wish to resign your role as my governess. Only think how disagreeable it will be for you to start a new position with a stranger—some willful, ill-trained child—and how awful for me the trial of a new governess! What if she objects to my study of nature? What if she tells Mama of my interest in physic?"

"You are full of alarms. What seems like misfortune today, may be considered an opportunity tomorrow. You must know in your heart that we are good friends and loyal companions, and let me remind you: you have many friends in Hunsford. Think of Miss Sullen and her sister, Miss Matilda—Tilly, as you have always called her—and even Miss Ormiston, who often tries your patience."

Anne slumped in her chair as if all the light in the world had gone out.

Miss Waygood offered encouragement rather than a reprimand for her charge's unladylike posture. "I have been gratified to watch you mature into a poised young lady from the noisy, rumbustious child I met nearly four years ago—you, a girl, more interested in the birth of piglets in the barn than learning to speak French in the drawing room. I have taught you most of what I know, not that it was ever drudgery, for you have a lively mind and natural curiosity. But this new phase of your life requires a different type of guidance."

"In other words, Mama is punishing you for my bad behavior at my aunt's." Anne sulked as the waiter set two cups, a pot of tea, and small containers of cream and sugar on the table.

Miss Waygood poured the steaming brew, dropped two sugar cubes in her cup, and stirred her drink. "I am not being punished for any undesirable behavior of yours or, indeed, for any lapse in my own behavior. In truth, Lady Catherine and I have spoken several times in recent months of my desire to obtain another position and of your need for a more experienced person."

"What do you mean? You have satisfied Mama by teaching me French, embroidery, drawing, and the pianoforte, while also encouraging my desire to know more of the natural sciences. What other experience do I require?"

"Dearest girl, you must know my meaning," admonished Miss Waygood. "You recall the epic poem we studied last summer. 'For Fate has wove the thread of life with pain, And twins ev'n from the birth, are Misery and Man.'" She paused to let those words sink in. "For all mankind, life's changes can be vexing, but that is the human condition. You are of an age where you must set aside childish pursuits and assume the roles of womanhood."

Anne's eyes widened on hearing this charge. A vision of Mr. Wickham's vulgar print came to mind, followed quickly by images of his teasing eyes and kissable lips. "You quote the *Odyssey*? I do not understand you."

"How many times has Lady Catherine spoken of your duty and your destiny? You will marry Mr. Darcy and become a great lady—*that* we know with certainty since your engage-ment was announced to the family. The mistress of Pemberley will have many duties, not only within the family, for you are expected to produce a male heir and manage the household with efficiency and charity, but also within the broader world, where you will entertain and forge alliances that enhance Mr. Darcy's status. The union of Pemberley and Rosings will secure the futures of both families." Miss Waygood turned to smile at a distinguished gentleman sitting close by who admired her pleasing form as he sipped his tea. "I will find a new position, perhaps here in London."

"With Mr. Dighurst?" Anne bit her lip as soon as the words were released.

Miss Waygood frowned at Anne's understanding. "That is none of your concern. It is only to be expected that we would become a little acquainted, considering the closeness of the Dighursts to the de Bourgh family. Let me reassure you: there is no intimacy between Mr. Dighurst and me. Now, I wish you to accompany me on an errand, but it requires a short walk, after which I shall escort you to Lady Anne's, where I understand an apology is in order."

Chapter 9

A Good Marriage

At Darcy House Miss Waygood informed the butler that she would return within the hour to call on Lady Anne and retrieve her charge. She patted Anne's arm before setting forth down the front steps.

Anne's breath quickened. She tried to muster her composure while shedding her pelisse and muff, which a footman gathered. "This way, Miss de Bourgh," Jacobs said sonorously. She followed him across the entry hall and up the stairs to the drawing room, thinking how glorious it would be to escape below-stairs, like she had done as a child; she might sample a fresh-baked biscuit in the cook's warm kitchen and pretend all was well with the world. Instead, she listened to Jacobs announce her arrival, her chin quivering as she blinked back tears in advance of her apology.

Thankfully, Fitzwilliam was nowhere to be seen.

"Dear Anne. I hope your walk was not too onerous, for I hear the wind has freshened. Come sit here." Lady Anne patted a sofa cushion. "Allow me to introduce you to Mrs. Stevens, my childhood friend and neighbor." Turning to her friend, she said, "You met my niece some ten or twelve years ago when she was but a girl."

"Indeed, I recall the occasion, although I daresay you do not," said the lady, smiling at Anne, "for you could not have been more than four or five years old at the time. Are you enjoying London?"

Their kindness confused Anne. "Yes, ma'am. There is much to entertain here."

To the questions that followed, she replied woodenly, wanting nothing more than to speak her apology, put the agony behind her, and return to her own bedchamber where she might collapse into Dobbie's care, but there was no ignoring her duty to behave as any young lady of her rank should behave when paying a social call. Fortunately, Mrs. Stevens stayed only a few minutes before taking her leave.

Lady Anne called to a footman. "If other callers should arrive, tell Jacobs to indicate that I am engaged and invite them to call again."

"As you wish, ma'am." The footman bowed and closed the drawing room door.

Anne's heart sank. Now that the dreaded moment was upon her she could hardly bring herself to look at her aunt, much less speak. She felt her aunt's warm hand squeeze her own.

"I know you have come to apologize, Anne, but I don't seek an apology. It is not at all necessary."

Anne stared at her aunt. "You don't want an apology? Have I not insulted you?"

"You expressed a heartfelt opinion regarding a decision made without your consent. To hear your opinion stated so frankly is exactly what I expected."

"But my behavior was horrid. I never considered whether my comment might hurt or distress you. I spoke without thinking."

"Do you wish to apologize to me?"

"Yes, I do! I am truly sorry if I caused you pain. It was never my intent to do so, for you have always shown me kindness. Your affection is a great joy to me."

"Then I accept your apology."

Anne was flummoxed by this turn of events. She had dreaded this conversation, almost to the point of being ill, and now the thing was done—without tears, without stammering excuses or painful recriminations. She had expressed her regret sincerely. Still, there were unanswered questions, beginning with the one uppermost in her thoughts: Did her aunt and uncle truly favor the engagement of their only son to his Kentish cousin? It would be a rude question to ask, especially after Lady Anne's gracious conduct.

"There is more to discuss, is there not?" asked Lady Anne, a hint of a smile on her lips.

Anne marveled at the differences between this sweet, complaisant woman and her mother. Where Lady Catherine was tall and big-boned, fond of sharing her opinions, and a captive of rank and title, Lady Anne was petite and polite, preferred her quiet country life, and seldom thought of *le beau ton*; she was a happy, busy chickadee to her older sister's more formidable sparrowhawk.

"Yes, I believe so," replied Anne. "How did you come to support my engagement to Fitzwilliam?"

"It is no mystery, for most families seek alliances that favor their prospects. In fact, your mother and I began discussing a marriage between our children before either of us married. On our side, your uncle and I view your marriage to Fitzwilliam not as a case of wishing to build a dynasty that will endure for centuries—we cannot be so conceited!—but rather as a desire to know that our son and you are situated securely and comfortably to face a changing world. We hope one day to enjoy a grandson—your son—and a daughter or two. Furthering our family line will strengthen our social position and consequence. But even that is not our main concern. What your uncle and I most want for Fitzwilliam is that he has the power to do good in the world. *That* is what we expect of him. The power to do good is best accomplished by a man of property who enjoys the counsel of wise friends and the affection of a wife who supports his endeavors." Lady Anne paused, her lips pursed as she studied her niece's face. "There is also the issue of your character. I believe you will be good for him."

"I? Good for Fitzwilliam? In what way?"

"Fitzwilliam is as fine a son as your uncle and I could ever hope for, but we sometimes wish he were less reserved. He does not make friends easily. In Derbyshire, that is no surprise, for there are few young men of our acquaintance who can challenge and inspire him. Indeed, we hope he will make two or three good friends at Cambridge, where there will be many young men of like mind and character. But marriage … marriage is altogether different. We expect his wife to be loyal to him, of course, to provide an heir, to respect him, and to help him achieve his goals. I believe you can do all of these things."

Sure of Anne's complete attention she added, "Only one concern remains: I am not convinced of your affection for him, by which I mean an affection beyond that which I know you feel for all of your cousins."

Anne stood on dangerous ground, for her aunt's comment was perilously close to the question her father had asked: Why did she not like Fitzwilliam? What could she reply, especially as she could not answer the question? It would be abominable to confess that she did not love Fitzwilliam as she thought a wife should. Nor, after gaining her aunt's approbation, could she be flippant about so sensitive a matter. How could she explain that she found her cousin Richard—and, dare she admit it, Mr. Wickham—more attractive than Fitzwilliam? How could she make sense of some ill-defined personal preference or vague hunch without hurting nearly everyone in her family? It would be like trying to explain why she preferred autumn over spring or asparagus to beets. Knowing she must reply, Anne chose her words carefully. "I possess every proper feeling for Fitzwilliam as a cousin, true enough, but I do not know whether my affection is sufficient to make a good marriage."

"I understand. Your heart does not flutter and leap at the mere thought of him. Is that not so?"

Anne nodded, not trusting herself to speak. One man made her heart flutter and leap, but it wasn't Fitzwilliam.

"You are still quite young, Anne, and imagine that love born of passion always endures. It does not. There are many kinds of love. A good marriage, a lasting marriage, relies less on passion and more on steady affection and respect."

Anne considered these words. How could marriage survive without passion? A marriage founded on simple affection and respect must surely end in boredom and discontent. The lack of passion between man and wife must corrode family life and even character. What was life without passion? What was marriage where man and wife behaved with politeness and reserve toward one another; where a studied formality or barely concealed tolerance was acceptable; where children were born of duty, not ardor? Surely such a union would bring no joy. She had only to study her parents' marriage to see the truth of her conclusion. This thought prompted a question. "Would it be impertinent of me to ask whether your marriage was arranged as my mother's was?"

"It is an impertinent question, but not an impudent one, and as I know you ask out of a sincere wish to further your understanding, I am willing to answer it. My marriage was not arranged in the same manner as your mother's. I was introduced to Mr. Darcy at a large house party hosted by my grandparents. The Fitzwilliams were fond of entertaining and often welcomed family and friends to spend several weeks at their country house during the hunting season. Mr. Darcy happened to be visiting a friend whose family estate was situated close by. We were frequently in each other's company over the next several weeks. His manners and charm and prospects impressed my parents, such that when he asked to pay his addresses to me, consent was given readily. I consider myself blessed to have met and married such a fine man, but we have had our share of sorrows and vexations. Such is life." She squeezed Anne's arm. "Let's not speak more of this now. Your uncle and I ask only that you work a little to know Fitzwilliam. You have hardly spent any time in his company, other than a few weeks here and there over the years, but now is your opportunity, for you will both be attending the same parties and balls. To know him a little better will make your heart rest easier."

Anne nodded her agreement to the plan but didn't believe a word of what her aunt said. Were there not similarities between the situation of Lady Anne's sister so many years ago and that of her niece today? Perhaps having the luxury of choice herself made it impossible for Lady Anne to appreciate the distress arising from having no right to choose at all.

Chapter 10

A Pleasing Prospect

"Are you determined to pursue this course? I do not expect a happy outcome if you go downstairs wearin' Miss Waygood's gift." Dobbie stood facing Anne and a little to one side, so as not to block Anne's view of her progress in the looking-glass as she restitched the lace on the bodice of Anne's gown.

"Miss Laycock performed a miracle with my hair. Do you not think so?" Anne tilted her head to view the comb encumbered with seed pearls that pinned her hair in place.

Dobbie recognized a diverting tactic when she saw one. "Aye, she has a deft touch and knows how to please, as do many Town hair-dressers, but Barton does just as well."

"You must be joking. Barton's gnarled hands are not nearly so nimble, although Mama prefers her hair-dressing to any other at Rosings. Dobbie, I wish you could have seen the Indian women in Covent Garden."

"Fie, Miss Anne! You cannot know anythin' of Covent Garden."

"But I do, for that is where Miss Waygood led me after we finished our tea. Near the Theatre Royal we turned off Long

Acre into a riot." Anne laughed to see the look on Dobbie's face. "Not a mean riot with bottle throwing and beatings, but a riot just the same. The street was such a jumble of carts and hackneys mixed with people, horses, and dogs that passage was nearly impossible. Surely every trade in the world operates there: tailors, boot-makers, drapers, cutlers. I watched a man stringing a violin, which I've never before seen in my life. And the smells! I fear the stench of the curriers and tripe-boilers still clings to my clothes. I wanted to browse the wire-workers' wares, but Miss Waygood said we had no time."

"It scares me to death to think of you two walkin' in that part of Town. Why, the place is thick with rufflers and sharpers and other such vermin. You might have been set upon, robbed, or kidnapped. And then where would we be?" Dobbie shook her head with murky imaginings of bodily violence, but her curiosity emerged in the absence of dire consequences. "What of the Indian women? What were they like?"

"They were charming." Anne found the entire adventure enchanting. The proprietor's gracious bow, the aroma of strange spices, and the stacks of brilliantly colored cottons and cashmere in nooks behind the counter were all marvelous. "The older woman, the wife of the proprietor, I believe, came forward and led us to a small table on one side. We were invited to be seated on cushioned stools. The younger woman, her daughter, disappeared through a shimmering curtain of beaded muslin and returned carrying a package, which she laid before me as if I were a courtesan of the Maharaja."

"As if you know anythin' of the Maharaja," joked Dobbie. "Good for nothin' foreigners."

"Their dresses were most unusual. One was as orange as a day lily; the other, forest green. Their gowns, if so they be called, draped and flowed in curious ways, and seemed somehow to form trousers."

"They wore men's trousers?" asked a stupefied Dobbie, whose knowledge of ladies' dress was drawn mainly from the environs of Scrag Bush on Kent's High Weald, where she was born, and Hunsford, where she had been married and expected to end her days. Anything more exotic than a bonnet and muslin gown was cause to wonder where the world was headed.

"Not precisely. It is difficult to describe. Such remarkable people thrive in that part of Town."

"How is it that Miss Waygood knew of this shop?"

Anne had not considered this question. Her governess was assuredly familiar with the area. Indeed, she must have known the Indian women, for their arrival had been anticipated. "I do not know, now that you ask, but her sister lives in Cheapside and may have told her of it.

"All the more reason to leave the shawl with me. I would not care to stand in your shoes if Lady Catherine learns you've been traipsin' around Covent Garden looking for Indians."

Anne refused to acknowledge the sense of Dobbie's argument.

After a minute of respectful silence, Dobbie said in her gentlest mothering tone: "Child, I wish you would not do this. It will only rile her ladyship and make trouble for yourself."

"I shall wear Miss Waygood's shawl. I can think of no greater compliment to give her. When our guests arrive, Mama will have little time for noting such trifles as a new shawl."

Dobbie pursed her lips, not being convinced by these fine words. Lady Catherine, she knew, had very particular ideas about what was proper for a young lady to wear, and a red paisley shawl adorned with tassels and smelling peculiar was not likely to secure her approval.

"Make sure my hem is even," said Anne, as she pulled the shawl across her shoulders and stood ramrod straight before the looking-glass. To her eye, the shawl's dusky reds and faded pinks did not overpower the golden hue of her dress. Its dangling fringe fell almost to her knees and made her feel mysterious.

Dobbie acquiesced but held her tongue, being full of apprehensions and imaginings.

Anne twirled once, pleased with the effect the shawl lent her figure. She kissed Dobbie's plump cheek, crossed the chamber without a backward glance, and tiptoed down the hall. Standing in the shadows at the top of the stairs, she feared Dobbie had the right of it. Already she felt remorse for the harsh tone she had dealt her maid.

What a gentle soul was Martha Dobbie. She had entered service at twelve years of age, married one of the de Bourgh family's coachmen, and raised five children at Rosings, of which two sons survived. Her life had not been easy this past year since her husband died of a malignant fever, and it pained Anne to see tears in those blue eyes and worry lines on her dear face. She had known no other maid and loved Dobbie for her sighs and pats, her gifts of affection and encouragement, her kindly scolding, and her comforting presence every day. Because she herself had no siblings, Dobbie's stories of life in Scrag Bush, where her parents farmed and raised four boys and three girls, were riveting, opening a window into a life Anne could barely imagine.

Believing Dobbie deserved a sweet-tempered mistress, Anne vowed to make amends on the morrow. At the moment she was anxious to catch a glimpse of Mr. Wickham.

Downstairs Sir Lewis and Lady Catherine welcomed their relations to Chidham House in good spirits.

Unlike many families, the holy cords binding the de Bourghs and the Darcys had not been bruised by anger, absence, or affection, and all felt free to enjoy themselves. Lady Catherine drew her sister to a sofa, where she delighted in sharing stories of her recent activities. "I heard much about Lady Melbourne at Mrs. Palmerson's rout. Poor woman, to have lost her younger daughter this summer. The child was only fourteen. Lady Melbourne is having quite a miserable time of it, I am told. Her remaining daughter, Emily, is nearly Anne's age and is said to be a pretty girl with excellent prospects. Have you met Miss Lamb? No matter—"

Lady Anne listened and asked questions, as was expected of her.

While Lady Catherine told tales of her social success, Lady Anne's eye flickered to Mr. Wickham, who was talking to her niece near the tea table.

Anne, unaware of her aunt's critical study, was trying not to laugh.

Wickham stood beside her, teacup in hand, and asked, "Did the witch cast a spell on you or threaten to toss you into her cauldron for our impudence in the library?"

"Don't call Mama a witch," Anne scolded half-heartedly as she picked up a biscuit.

"What would you call her? A toad? A weasel? A Tower gaoler? A horrid—"

"I wouldn't—oh, stop!"

"Come, we both know she is not one to forgive and forget. Punishment is more her style." Wickham plucked a tea cake from a silver tray. "What penance does she demand in payment for your sin?"

Anne winced at so direct an understanding and did not mention Miss Waygood's forthcoming departure. "She told me to stop encouraging you, as if I could. You don't need much goading to get me in trouble."

Wickham chuckled at this sally.

"True. I enjoy the sport, for you are wonderfully biddable. I need only toss a musket ball in your path to scatter your wits."

He popped the entire cake into his mouth and washed down the treat with a great gulp of tea.

"What an unkind thing to say. I had not thought you so mean spirited."

"You little country bumpkin. Surely you know I am teasing you. There is no better way to make your eyes flash and spark. I believe you are about to give me a scold for my insolence."

Anne gave him a stern look to dampen his teasing. "I am not, although you deserve one. Tell me what you think about going up to Cambridge. Shall you do well in your studies?"

A strange grin graced Wickham's face. "I believe I shall do very well, indeed."

Anne observed the glow in his eyes. "What do you mean?"

"Only that I expect to be busy."

"You mean to compete with Fitzwilliam, then. He will surpass you in every subject, I daresay, for he is a natural scholar."

"That was unkind. I cannot compete with Fitz—"

"Don't call him Fitz. You know he hates that name."

"I cannot compete with Fitz and learned long ago that I gain nothing by appearing to best him. My parentage places me well beneath him and, even though I am his father's godson, he will never be my brother or friend. He believes himself superior to me in every respect, but then, he has been coddled and flattered all of his life. He does not feel the hand of Fate—a fickle woman, if ever there was one—and has never known hardship. He expects to rise in society, to feel its blessing, and to receive its praise for little more than a fine countenance and good manners. Fitz is—"

"—coming in this direction!" Anne exclaimed in a panicky whisper.

Wickham turned. "Ah, Fitz. We were just speaking of you."

Fitzwilliam's manner was brusk. "My father wishes to speak with you."

Wickham thrust his teacup at Fitzwilliam and winked at Anne.

Fitzwilliam set the unwanted item on a tray with a clatter and accepted a cup for himself. He blew across the hot brew and surveyed the room.

Anne sought to master herself. She seldom felt comfortable in her cousin's presence, sometimes losing all her wits and becoming strangely shy and tongue-tied, as now. Why could she not find the ease with him that she felt with Mr. Wickham? Was Fitzwilliam formal with her because she was so with him? To her he was always rather reserved and formidable, and she was forever struggling to find something of interest to say to him. Since any mention of their engagement would be beyond the pale, she must find an innocuous topic that would neither offend nor surprise. Just as she fixed to ask whether his younger sister, Georgiana, would attend the card party, he said, "Pray excuse me," and walked off. Feeling abandoned, Anne forced herself to eat the biscuit. She was rescued by her aunt, who signaled to her. "Come, sit with me a few minutes," said Lady Anne.

Anne complied, wondering whether her aunt had seen the awkward moment between her son and niece.

"I have been admiring your shawl. Is it new?"

"Yes, thank you. Miss Waygood presented it to me yesterday."

"It is quite a fine piece and suits you very well. Now, I wish to tell you of some news that may interest you. Yesterday I visited Lord and Lady Matlock and met two of your aunt's relations—a niece and nephew, the children of your aunt's sister. Miss Maria Derrythorpe and her younger brother James have been sent to London to stay with the Fitzwilliams while their siblings recover from the measles. This being their first visit to Town, they are excited at the prospect of enjoying London's pleasures in your and your cousins' company. You shall meet them at next week's card party. I believe you will enjoy their company, for you have much in common with them."

"A pleasing prospect, to be sure," Anne said, feeling obligated to show some enthusiasm over accepting two foreigners into her family circle. "Do you know of any particular activities that will appeal to them?"

"I suspect everything will excite them. They have traveled down from Clun, a rustic village in the southern reaches of Shropshire, and shall find much to entertain them here."

Lady Catherine, who thrived on the glitter and gossip of society and valued status and connections above all things, interposed her opinion and reported their heritage. "Miss and Mr. Derrythorpe's father, Sir Thomas Derrythorpe, is a sheep farmer, but there is no shame in that, for the de Bourghs built their profits on sheep farming in Saxon times. Sir Thomas's wife is a close cousin of Lord Staireford, whose family seat lies in Wiltshire, not far from your uncle Matlock's seat." Her smile was one of satisfaction on finding a noteworthy connection, however tenuous, between the children of a sheep farmer and her aristocratic brother, Edwin Augustus Fitzwilliam, 2nd Earl of Matlock. "Although Miss Derrythorpe is only a few months older than yourself, you have the greater experience in society and can show her how to behave with dignity and decorum when in polite company."

"I shall do my best, Mama," she said, hardly attending to her mother's counsel for being curious about what uncle Darcy was saying to Mr. Wickham.

Chapter 11

No Mere Pretty Girl

Lady Catherine praised to the sky Miss Derrythorpe's many charms: "She is a very pretty girl, only a few months older than you, and so accomplished. She plays the pianoforte and sings beautifully."

When pressed, her ladyship admitted to never having heard Miss Derrythorpe perform, but she was confident Lady Matlock's niece had received the highest training.

"I am not fond of my brother's wife—your aunt Fitzwilliam makes much of her connections and would have us believe she dines at Carlton House every week—what nonsense!—but I am not so prejudiced as to deny her affection for her sister's children. Lady Derrythorpe must manage seven children, the youngest four of whom have taken to their beds with measles. It is no wonder she accepted Lady Matlock's invitation to send her two eldest to London. Given the family's circumstances, it must do the children good to be seen with the Fitzwilliams and enjoy a dignified society not found in Shropshire. I'm told their manners are very proper, which does them credit." Lady Catherine expounded on the young persons' good fortune in having such gracious relations before telling Anne, "Few young ladies are as promising and popular as Miss Derrythorpe, and her younger brother, only a few months younger than yourself, is growing into a most congenial young man."

As if these words were not sufficient, her ladyship entered Anne's bedchamber while Dobbie was laying out her clothes for the card party. "Take care with your hair and gown," Lady Catherine warned, giving Dobbie a stern eye before staring at Anne, "for we cannot have you looking a dowdy rustic. As it is, I fear Miss Derrythorpe's beauty will put you in the shade. Still, she will be a good companion for you, if you will try to win her friendship." Scanning Anne's bedchamber with practiced eyes her ladyship added, "Do not wear that awful shawl this evening. Its smell is most peculiar."

These comments made Anne peevish all through the carriage ride to her uncle's house in St. James's Square.

Why could she not wear her new shawl? It was elegant and fashionable and suited her coloring. And why must she befriend Miss Derrythorpe? The girl would likely prove to be dull as an old paring knife—a fault more fatal than beauty. One could not be forced into friendship. Consider Tilly and her older sister, Margaret, the daughters of Mr. Sullen, the current rector of Hunsford parish. After Mrs. Sullen died in childbirth, at a time when the girls were quite small—Tilly was only four years old and Margaret, six—Sir Lewis offered Mr. Sullen the Hunsford parish living, believing he could make no better choice for the village than his dear friend from Oxford. Within a month of the Sullens settling into the parsonage, Anne barely tolerated Margaret, who was her own age, but adored Tilly, who was two years younger. Indeed, since their early acquaintance Tilly and Anne had been inseparable and thought of themselves as sisters, which only proved that friendship blossomed unbidden.

The slashing rain and jostling coaches on London's busy streets failed to cheer, but on entering the grand hall of Matlock House Anne's mood rose.

She preceded her parents up the wide staircase to where her uncle stood waiting, a grin on his face. "How charming you look, dear niece. Is that a new gown?"

"Yes, thank you, uncle. Miss Waygood selected the muslin for me, and you know she has impeccable taste."

"Of course she does. Look how well she favors you," he said, with a glint of mischief in his eyes.

Anne could only laugh at this overstatement. She was fond of her mother's brother. Lord Matlock had a tall, imposing figure and a square face ruled by unruly eyebrows and long sideburns turning white. His informal manner, tempered with dry humor, made him popular in the House of Lords, where he was building a reputation among the Tories as a nimble political thinker. No doubt there would be open discussions at supper on various party concerns.

Turning, Lord Matlock said, "Ah, sister, you look well, and Sir Lewis—come in, come in. Let's go into the saloon, where a fire and refreshments await you. The Darcys and Mr. Wickham are there, along with my own sons, and I shall introduce you to my wife's niece and nephew. We are a merry group."

A clutch of relations greeted the de Bourghs as they entered the well-lit room.

Lady Anne and uncle Darcy, standing with their young daughter, Georgiana, bestowed kisses and well-wishes. Georgiana clutched her mother's hand before dropping an unsteady curtsy.

Anne stooped down, saying to her young cousin, "You look charming this evening—the very picture of fashion."

Georgiana impulsively hugged Anne's neck, which tickled everybody.

"Gracious heaven, you are strong as an ox!" Anne teased. "Have you been wrestling with Fitzwilliam?"

"Girls don't wrestle," Georgiana said shyly.

"Indeed, they don't, and your brother is far too refined to wrinkle your gown," Anne replied, giving the child's hands a squeeze. She accepted greetings from a bemused Fitzwilliam and Lord Matlock's elder son and heir, Charles, who bowed formally. Next Lord Matlock's younger son, Richard, stepped forward to press her hand. "Wrestling seems more *your* style, cousin." His crooked grin charmed.

Anne smiled at Richard's joking manner before submitting to Mr. Wickham's greeting. "Delighted, as always, cousin Anne. I hope to entertain you at the card table this evening."

"It would be my pleasure." Her stomach fluttered at the sight of his tousled curls and bright eyes.

Lord Matlock said to Anne, "Allow me to introduce you to Miss Maria Derrythorpe and her younger brother James. They are newly arrived in Town and look forward to making your acquaintance."

Mr. Derrythorpe's friendly manner and ready smile beguiled, but Anne's courage nearly failed when faced with the much-praised lady herself, for she instantly perceived that her own person was rude as a thistle compared with this English rose. Miss Derrythorpe was no mere pretty girl, but a true beauty. Her bright eyes seemed overly large in her small face and shone nearly black in their hue—almost as black as an hussar's hat—while her glossy ebony curls, gathered with pink ribbons, fell from the crown of her head. Her complexion was so fair as to be almost translucent, and in form she was dainty, with prettily formed hands and pale-skinned shoulders.

Anne forced a pleasing countenance, feeling frumpy as an old maid; but no sooner had their formal curtsies been tendered than the girl bestowed a bewitching smile and said, "I am pleased to meet you and hope we shall be friends, for I know not a soul in London, other than my aunt's family and my brother. You appear to be just the sort of friend to guide me, for I understand you have often visited this grand city."

Unaccustomed to being greeted with such friendly condescension, Anne succumbed to sincerity and realized Miss Derrythorpe was not more handsome than Tilly, whose beauty was much admired in Hunsford. Tilly was taller and bigger boned than Miss Derrythorpe, but few women possessed the wavy, chestnut-hued hair that was Tilly's crowning glory.

Reminding herself not to be intimated by her new acquaintance's looks, Anne entered into a discussion of Miss Derrythorpe's first impressions of London and the best haberdashery for lace and gloves—Harding, Howell and Company in Pall Mall, without a doubt—until the card games began.

The Beauty, as Anne thought of her, insisted on securing her new friend to her table, along with Charles and Fitzwilliam, where she proved her skill at whist and complained of having two determined adversaries: "My friends in Clun are not so skilled at cards as you, Miss de Bourgh, and Charles. Indeed, had I not partnered Mr. Darcy I could not claim a win!"

When the card game broke up for supper, the Beauty pulled Anne to the window. "Why does your cousin stare at me? Does he find me disagreeable? Do I offend him?"

Anne surveyed her relations. "Do you mean Mr. Darcy?"

"For all his attractive features, Mr. Darcy is a well-formed man but a bit intimidating, don't you think? I speak of your other cousin," Miss Derrythorpe said a little breathlessly.

Anne knew she could not be speaking of Richard.

Stocky in form, Richard's brown eyes hinted at a somewhat mischievous personality, which to Anne's way of thinking more than compensated for a smile marred by several crooked teeth. He generally looked as though he were thinking of some new devilment, which demeanor often got him into trouble with his mother and sometimes annoyed Lady Catherine.

Nor could she be speaking of Charles, who seemed always to be frowning, except when he talked about hounds and horses. The appearance of neither cousin could compare with Fitzwilliam's imposing stature and fine features.

Miss Derrythorpe's eyes flicked to Mr. Wickham. "That cousin."

Anne felt a moment's disquiet. "You are mistaken. Mr. Wickham is no cousin. He is my uncle's godson and the son of his former steward. He grew up on the Darcy family estate and is quite intimate with the family, but you would do well to keep your distance from him."

"I perfectly comprehend your hint but must object to your advice. Many a man of humble birth has proven his character and been accepted by society. In Mr. Wickham's case, his charming manners and merry eye are likely to secure his advancement, and failing that, there is his association with the Darcy family, which will serve him well." Miss Derrythorpe looked thoughtful. "I believe he knows exactly what I'm wearing under this muslin gown."

Anne glanced with alarm at Mr. Wickham, who smiled at her as if she were the only person in the room. She felt her cheeks redden.

"All the more reason," she warned her new friend, "to keep your distance. My governess is forever reminding me that he will not make a suitable husband, since his prospects depend to a great extent on my uncle's generosity."

Miss Derrythorpe's shining eyes glinted in the candlelight. "It very much depends on whether one wants a suitable husband. There are many kinds of husbands, are there not?"

Anne knew not what to reply to this odd statement and was relieved to enter the dining room for supper.

At table there was much discussion about London's many amusements. Mr. Derrythorpe, who could not help his awkward age, being some moments a lively schoolboy and other times, an awkward young man on the cusp of adulthood, was all for visiting the Tower.

"I read about the wild beasts in my London pocket-guide. They have names!" he exclaimed. "There's Miss Fanny Howe—a lioness named for Admiral Howe's daughter—and Young Hector and Miss Jenny … We must go. It costs only a shilling to see these magnificent creatures."

"James, how can you choose smelly animals over fashion?" asked Miss Derrythorpe, seemingly all out of countenance with him. "You would have me bemire my boots for the misery of studying wild beasts. I would much prefer a drive down Rotten Row. Mama told me the Town dandies take a turn there in the morning. Why, we might see Mr. Brummell himself or perhaps a duke or duchess."

"What? Choose a dandy over the Tower lions?" protested the younger Derrythorpe. "Anybody can spy a dandy walking in Bond Street or Piccadilly. The lions, on the other hand, are exceptional. When are we ever likely to see a lion?"

While the siblings argued across the table, Wickham whispered to Anne, "Mr. Derrythorpe is not aware that many predators walk in Bond Street and Piccadilly."

"I was thinking the same thing myself."

"That does not surprise me, for you are more forward in the world than many young persons. Your aunt's relatives are mere country cherubs and appear quite lost in Town. I am surprised they have no chaperon or governess dancing to their wishes. Perhaps Miss Waygood can be imposed upon to escort them."

"I believe Mr. Derrythorpe has been charged with chaperoning his sister. He must be thought sufficiently mature to do so, although he seems young for the responsibility."

"What do you think of his sister?"

"She is very pretty and has pleasing manners. I like her. She will have a dozen men at her feet within a week, including Fitzwilliam, who seemed to succumb to her charm over cards. I have never known him to be so loquacious." Anne studied Mr. Wickham's face in the candlelight. "Perhaps you will be her next conquest." She was seldom so directly provoking in her dealings with him.

Wickham smirked at her tease. "She has beauty, I allow, but is missing a quality you have in abundance."

"What might that be?"

"Sweet virtue."

He gave a low chuckle and turned to speak to Richard.

Chapter 12

The Art of Love-Making

On the Thursday following, Lady Catherine and her daughter returned to Matlock House.

"Ma'am. Miss de Bourgh," said Lord Matlock's butler, Higson, as he supervised the footman gathering the ladies' coats and muffs. "Lady Matlock awaits you upstairs."

For Lady Catherine every invitation to her brother's house was a home-coming, a reminder of a girlhood spent traveling between the Fitzwilliam's family seat in Wiltshire and this house in London's most prestigious square.

In the front drawing room she had danced many a country dance; served tea to her dearest friend, Miss Pottinger (now deceased); flirted with two handsome brothers, the sons of Lord Edgeworth; and was introduced to and hoped to marry Mr. Urson, the eldest son of a baron, who murdered his family's hopes by eloping with the daughter of a common London alderman before the settlements were signed. All these years later her blood still boiled at the memory. After that scheme collapsed she became engaged to Sir Lewis, which was not a topic she cared to dwell on.

She swept up the curving staircase, her hand brushing the railing. In this house the weight of family ties reached back in time more than seventy years. Built for the Fitzwilliam family in the 1720's, Matlock House was situated across the square from Norfolk House. Always sensible of the honor of sharing St. James's Square with the Duke of Norfolk and other esteemed aristocratic families, her ladyship all but nodded her approval of Fortune's blessing as she passed under her father's portrait hanging majestically at the top of the stairs. Augustus Henry Charles Fitzwilliam, 1st Earl of Matlock, had not been an easy man to love, but he had bequeathed his resilience and steely will to his elder daughter, who was proud to wear his stamp.

"Welcome, sister, niece. It is good to see you both looking well." After the ladies settled themselves and conversed on desultory topics, Lady Matlock said to Anne, "Maria has a proposal for you."

"Oh, yes," said Miss Derrythorpe. "I have been anxious to know whether you would be so good as to accompany my brother and me to see the wild animals at the Tower. James assures me of their being most curious. The weather is fine, if a little damp, and we shall have time to enjoy hot chocolate afterwards."

Anne suppressed her surprise. "I would be delighted to join you, for I haven't visited the menagerie for several years."

"An excellent idea," interposed Lady Catherine. "Miss Waygood shall escort you. We brought her to Town just for this purpose, and I know she would be delighted to chaperon you all. Indeed, what else does she have to do?"

While the tea table was being laid, a discussion ensued of London's magnificent parks, which the young people would enjoy visiting. When the conversation turned to an account of Lady Carlington's daughter being now engaged to the eldest son of Sir Henley Hapsford, Miss Derrythorpe drew Anne to the window seat overlooking the square.

"I cannot abide conversations about people I neither know nor care about. Here we can enjoy ourselves in private."

"I thought you did not care to visit the Tower. You seemed taken against the idea at the card party, calling it a misery."

"What can I do when my brother is so very persuasive and persistent?" Miss Derrythorpe gave a pretty shrug. "If I do not accompany him, he will plague me for days and write our father with tales of my failing to follow his instructions."

"You were commanded to accompany your brother on an excursion to see the lions?"

"Lord, no! I was warned to be agreeable and to join my brother in his various pursuits during our stay in Town, which is most provoking, for my interests are nothing like his. You are fortunate not to have such responsibilities."

"You may be right, but I sometimes wish for a sister or two. It would be pleasing to have ready and familiar companionship. My dear friend, Miss Sullen, whose father is the rector in Hunsford, is very like a sister to me."

"You know nothing of the matter. My younger sisters are horrid creatures, always stealing my jewelry and pestering to borrow my ribbons. Does Miss Sullen listen at doors, read your journal, and tattle to your governess behind your back? I very much doubt it. It is better to have a good friend like Miss Sullen than a real sister. Brothers are better than sisters, in any event, for they tend to leave one alone."

"True, I am ignorant of such matters, but if I can't have a sister, then I wouldn't mind having a brother, especially if he were like cousin Richard. He makes me laugh."

"Richard is nice enough, but terribly plain, and I do not care for his satirical eye. I prefer a different sort of character—a handsome man, at least. And you? Are you excited by your engagement to Mr. Darcy? I was surprised to learn of it, for I had thought he was flirting with me at the card table. I must have been mistaken, for why would he flirt with me when he is engaged to you?" Miss Derrythorpe tittered.

The astute question rattled Anne's composure, for she had thought much the same thing. Fitzwilliam's face softened whenever he looked at his pretty partner. Indeed, he grinned like a regular mooncalf at every little thing Miss Derrythorpe said and was himself talkative and spirited, which manners were contrary to his usual style.

"I saw that he admired you," Anne admitted, "but then, you are uncommonly pretty, and most men, I believe, cannot help responding to beauty with frank admiration."

"That is certainly true. Every lady is pleased to be the subject of admiration. I never tire of receiving such regard myself, especially when bestowed by handsome men of good fortune like Mr. Darcy. What sort of husband do you expect him to be?"

Anne knew a moment's terror, for she dared not speak her mind. "I expect he'll do his duty."

To this honest confession Miss Derrythorpe hid a girlish giggle behind her hand. "Well, that may be true, but it doesn't speak to his regard! Have you given no thought to whether he will be a good lover? That is the important question."

A blush crept up Anne's throat. She stared down into the street, seemingly fascinated by the antics of two energetic spaniels on leash, and wondered how to respond. Such an intimate, indelicate topic should not be discussed between two ladies who had only recently been introduced, nor could it be explored with any prudence in her aunt's drawing room, however grand its proportions and furnishings.

She recalled once having a similar conversation with Tilly when the two of them were settled in the parsonage's cozy parlor, teacups in hand, at a time when Mr. Sullen was out visiting a sick parishioner. Their discussion of the intimate aspects of married life was naturally more speculative than affirmative, for neither of them had the least idea what they were talking about. In the present case misdirection seemed the safest course.

"What did you mean when you spoke of there being different kinds of husbands? It seems to me that one husband is much like another. Each has his own foibles, his own interests, and his own happy pleasures. I suppose some husbands are naturally more agreeable than others, and a wife must always hope for a complacent and likable husband. Of course, a husband and father must be of good moral character, especially for his children, else all society would be threatened by undesirable conduct. What more is there?"

A tinkling peal burst forth from Miss Derrythorpe. She leaned forward, saying in hushed tones, "Forgive me, I had no idea you did not understand the role of a husband in siring an heir."

"Of course I understand the natural order, for I have seen the stallion mating with the mare. There must be similarities among the different species." Anne refrained from commenting on the hounds she once watched mating in the Rosings stable yard. They stayed bound to one another for more than half an hour, which astonished her no end.

"No doubt," the Beauty replied, "but I want a husband who is handsome and lively and a good lover, else what is the point of being married if you take no pleasure in his love-making?"

"These are desirable qualities, I am sure, but how can a lady know anything of her husband's love-making before marriage? She is not allowed to be alone with her intended. Her parents or guardian will insist on a governess or maid accompanying her everywhere, sometimes even after she is engaged." Anne glanced at her mother and aunt to satisfy herself of their not being interested in the ludicrous conversation taking place in the window seat.

"Any lady, with a little effort and imagination, can contrive a private interlude with her intended or lover," countered Miss Derrythorpe. "One must be discreet, of course, as misery is the outcome if she is caught by a sibling or busybody."

Anne stared with frank skepticism. "Have *you* managed it?"

Miss Derrythorpe's sly smile hinted at her probable answer. "It takes only a little gumption to arrange it. The trick is not to appear too interested in having a private *tête-à-tête*, for the last thing you want is to put everybody out of countenance over the smallest indiscretion. An ardent look will let your lover know of your desire. He will respond in kind and arrange a meeting."

"An ardent look?" Anne pictured trying out various looks on Fitzwilliam: the petulant pout, the coy smile, the raised eyebrow. She predicted a puzzled, frowning countenance on her cousin's face if she gave him any of these artful poses.

"Have you tried meeting Mr. Darcy privately? Your families are together often enough to make it easy to contrive."

"I have not," said Anne, shrinking at the idea.

"That is unfortunate. When you contrive to be alone with him, you can test his love-making. It is the easiest thing in the world, for young men are often thinking of it." Seeing Anne's blank stare, Miss Derrythorpe snickered behind her hand. "You are truly a child, aren't you? At the very least you will want to learn whether he knows how to kiss properly."

An image of Mr. Wickham's face filled Anne's head. His wide mouth, while not in the common style, looked very kissable. "Yes, I can imagine how that might be important, but what if he kisses poorly?"

She could barely keep from laughing at their absurd conversation, for it had much of the farce about it.

"Then you cannot marry him! A lady should never accept less than what she wants in the way of love-making."

Anne was compelled to protest.

"Your advice is not practical. Many ladies, myself included, are expected to submit to their family's wishes and marry a man chosen for them, in which case they must strive to accept him, whether his love-making be good or bad. What can a lady do when she is obligated to marry a man whose character and habits she barely knows? Oftentimes the couple meet only two or three times before the wedding. In such cases there is no opportunity to assess his love-making before the knot is tied."

She thought of her parents' arranged marriage. How awkward to have conjugal relations with someone you barely knew. Yet this situation arose frequently among newly wedded couples of her station.

She tried to imagine Fitzwilliam leading her into the bridal chamber after their wedding. She would be chaste and must submit to him, after which she would know something of his love-making. Of course, she could draw no comparisons with other lovers, whereas he likely might. This thought terrified her and served to strengthen her vow to marry only for love in case she herself proved to be a terrible lover. A lady, after all, could have no confidence in her skill beforehand, whereas a man would likely be experienced. Surely it is best to marry for love, she thought, to find the one man who adores you, overlooks your deficiencies, and values your many fine qualities. She was moved to address this issue.

"There also remains the possibility that a lady might reject a good and decent man whose love-making does not please her but whose other merits make him worthy. Would you have her reject him only because he is not a good lover? If she wants children, she must learn to overcome any aversion to her husband's love-making, else what purpose does marriage serve?"

"You speak of a true tragedy." Miss Derrythorpe pulled herself up to assert her authority. "Given your situation, consider this: when next you are in company with Mr. Darcy, give him a tender look and he will understand you."

"I believe I lack the courage for it."

"You will be proven wrong, for it is the most natural thing in the world."

There was no truth in this statement so far as Anne could tell.

Chapter 13

A Lion's Roar

Mr. Derrythorpe's boyish enthusiasm led the way, and the party of young people, with Miss Waygood acting as a chaperon, now found themselves approaching Great Tower Hill. The carriage ride was as much an adventure as anything, since the Derrythorpes, new to London's marvels, exclaimed at every sight: "Look at that poor hunchback!—Oh, a fight has broken out between two wagoners.—Did you see the pearls on that crimson turban?—These London streets … My liver is half-jostled to death.—How funny, a sheep has escaped."

Their excitement infected everybody, such that when Lord Matlock's carriage disgorged its passengers, they were all in a jubilant mood and surprised to see Mr. Wickham. He stepped forward, smiling at Miss Waygood. "Do I trespass on your good humor by accompanying you today? I truly hope not, for I am tired of being indoors and wish to be entertained."

Miss Waygood's endorsement was tepid, at best, but she could not refuse him.

While Mr. Derrythorpe exhorted his sister and the others to hurry across the grounds, Wickham fell behind with Anne. "I am sure you noticed how proper were my manners in speaking with your governess. She is a handsome woman with a fine figure, and were I not so fond of you, dear cousin, I might be tempted to seek her favor. What say you to the idea? Can I make her fall in love with me?"

"It would do you no good to try," Anne warned, not liking his rattling style.

"Oh? Does she have a lover? If so, then he is a most fortunate man."

"I cannot speak to her private affairs, but you must realize she is not as naive as I. In her book you are not to be trusted."

"Oh-ho! Am I as bad as that? Surely I can claim at least one redeeming quality: I make you laugh. That is a gift beyond measure, is it not?"

His boyish grin won her heart and made her disposed to treat him kindly.

"True, but just as often you tease and goad. How unpredictable you are, like a summer storm. Come. Miss Waygood wonders why we dawdle." She had caught Miss Waygood's disapproving look and so tripped across the broad expanse to join her companions approaching the stone tower.

The small group merged with other well-dressed visitors eager for a glimpse of the King's stronghold. They had missed the morning's opening ceremony in which the yeoman porter unlocked the several gates with the governor's keys, as had been done for hundreds of years, but they eagerly pressed on. A strange mix of sounds and smells rode the crisp morning air.

"What is that awful odor?" cried Miss Derrythorpe as she stared at the massive stone fortress.

Wickham, standing behind her, cautioned, "It is the smell of the wild male." Seeing Miss Waygood's scowl, he rushed to add, "By which I mean the lion and the tiger. The animals are housed there in Lion Tower."

"This way!" called Mr. Derrythorpe. "The beasts are straight ahead." He pulled his sister along the stone passageway and approached a large door above which the figure of a lion was affixed. "We must ring the bell for the keeper. Have your shillings at hand."

All were ready when the door opened.

The keeper, a man middle-aged in years but fresh in manner, grinned upon the threshold. He was stout and jowly with over-large eyes and fleshy lips. Wiping his thick fingers on his knee-length, leather jerkin, he boasted, "You have arrived at a good time. The yard has few visitors as yet this brisk morning. You must first pay a twelver for the privilege, and then you shall b'hold such creatures as you have nev'r seen 'afore."

He gave Miss Derrythorpe an appreciative look. "You ain't scar'd now?" he teased as he counted the coins and pushed them into a leather pouch slung low on his hips. "No need to be cow-hearted, I'm sure, for they ain't hungry yet."

He chuckled as Miss Derrythorpe put a handkerchief to her nose and allowed him to lead her forward into the dim interior.

Anne herself felt a little timid on entering the gloom.

A large yard dominated the center of the circular tower. Several other visitors stood observing the animals. Ranged around the perimeter were ten or twelve chambers, each set under an arched ceiling and measuring about twelve feet high. Wooden shutters had been opened on several dens, revealing sturdy iron gratings, behind which the beasts prowled restlessly.

"My name is Bullock, a just and proper name, seeing as how the King sees me fit to corral these wild beasts," said the keeper, casting a friendly eye over the young cohort. "First, you see the animals in their upper cages, which, being 'bout level wi' the eye, gives you a good look at 'em. During the day they are kept up here; at night they're moved to the low cage. Let me make Miss Nancy known to you," he said, stepping toward a cage. "She's a leopardess and very tame—a gift from Sir Charles Mallet. No sweeter creature lives in these parts."

He stood back to allow his visitors a good view, before saying, "Over here you see Harry, a tiger from Bengal. Don't fear he'll grabble you, for he is also tame. Indeed, he's right fond of my little terrier, Charlie, who's off chasing rats this very hour. The two of them play together and Harry nev'r nips at Charlie. It's right funny to see. Now, here are the great lions." He waved his hand expressively. "Miss Fanny Howe is named for a daughter of Lord Howe. Miss Fanny wos whelped on the same day his lordship, who wos then Admiral of the Fleet, whipped the French at sea. That be June first of the year 1794, as I'm sure ye all recollect."

"The battle known as the Glorious First of June," added Wickham. He seemed not to notice Miss Waygood's or Anne's startled look.

"Very good. The gentleman knows his history," said Mr. Bullock. "Over here you'll see Young Hector and Miss Jenny, all fine animals, although they aren't so fond of our damp London winters. They both be three years old and come all the way from the Gulf of Persia."

Mr. Bullock took great care describing the lions' habits, what they were fed, and how they were exercised every day.

Anne listened with only one ear, for she was observing Mr. Wickham whispering to Miss Waygood and Miss Derrythorpe. While demonstrating some unfathomable action or object with his hands, the ladies laughed, their bonnets bobbing in agreement. When Mr. Wickham raised his eyes to meet hers, she spied the devilish look behind his grin and a warmth in his eyes. Her heart soared to feel his amiability.

"Come look at this one," Mr. Derrythorpe called to Anne.

Mr. Bullock, hearing the invitation, followed the pair to the next den. "Now that is Miss Peggy, our black leopardess. She hails from the Coast of Malabar and is our most special sight, for everybody be curious about her black spots."

Anne had never beheld such raw animal power, and this was a mere female. She stood transfixed as the creature paced the small cell, its shoulders rippling with each step. Its yellow eyes glowed with sultry resentment or boredom.

"She is beautiful," said Mr. Derrythorpe. "Her coat shines like silk. Wouldn't you agree?"

"Yes," said Anne, "and those eyes, they—"

A raucous roar came from their left, followed by a shriek. Anne jumped at the commotion and turned to see Miss Derrythorpe collapse in a dead faint into Mr. Wickham's arms.

Mr. Wickham did what any gentleman would do: he swept the young lady off her feet, maneuvered his way through the small crowd, and carried her slim figure through the middle tower and across the moat.

"Where are you taking her?" asked an anxious Miss Waygood as she tried matching her stride to his.

"Into the Tower grounds, which has a low stone wall where she can sit and recover."

"Oh, my head—" Miss Derrythorpe moaned as she struggled in Mr. Wickham's arms.

"If you will be still, miss," commanded Wickham, "I can carry you more easily." He continued down the lane, passed alongside the tall stone wall of the inner quadrangle and turned under the open portcullis of the Bloody Tower.

His companions followed on his heels.

Anne observed Miss Derrythorpe placing her arms around Mr. Wickham's neck. Mr. Derrythorpe snorted. "That girl is more trouble than a monkey in the dining room."

"You think her faint was faked?" asked an incredulous Anne. It never occurred to her that a lady would do such a thing on purpose. She certainly had not the courage for it.

"Nothing she does surprises me."

"Rest here," Miss Waygood was saying, as Mr. Wickham set Miss Derrythorpe on the stone wall. "You will feel better presently."

Miss Derrythorpe looked up at her rescuer. "Thank you, sir. I was quite overcome."

"The lion's roar startled you. I daresay it was calling a greeting to you, knowing he cannot expect to see another lady as pretty as you today."

Miss Waygood, not liking the direction of Mr. Wickham's conversation, called to Mr. Derrythorpe: "Be of use, if you please, and call the carriage. Do you know where to find it?"

"Yes, ma'am," he cried and took off through the crowd of visitors milling around the White Tower.

After a few minutes, Miss Waygood said, "Your color has returned. Can you walk out to the street?"

"I believe so. I'm sorry to be such trouble. I don't know what came over me."

"Take my arm," said Wickham, stepping forward. Miss Derrythorpe gave him a radiant smile.

Anne admired Mr. Wickham's gallantry, so solicitous was he of Miss Derrythorpe's welfare, but she disliked the ease with which he rescued the Beauty. Had her fainting fit been contrived? No, she could not believe so, for as the small group threaded their way through the crowd and emerged into the western square, Miss Derrythorpe seemed genuinely ill.

"Do not exert yourself, but rest and recover," commanded Miss Waygood after Mr. Wickham handed her into the carriage. "We shall take you back to Lord Matlock's house where you will be more comfortable."

"I am sorry to miss viewing the leopardess," Miss Derrythorpe said before slumping against the squabs, quite done in.

Chapter 14

Ants and Others

"There's Mr. Derrythorpe," said Anne, responding to his wave. She watched him push through a throng of people clustered around the western entrance to St. Paul's Cathedral. His boyish grin carried him through the crowd, bringing to mind an image of her cousin Richard. "I wonder why Miss Derrythorpe does not accompany him."

"Perhaps she has not recovered from her ordeal," said Miss Waygood.

Anne glanced sideways at her governess, whose tone suggested doubt about the Beauty's fainting spell.

"Miss de Bourgh, Miss Waygood. I have confirmed the price of admission: four pence for access to the outdoor galleries, which is precisely the amount stated in the pocket-guide, and an additional fee to see the body of the church. Not too dear, I hope. We should also view the curiosities, else why come all this way to see Wren's great achievement—at an extra charge of two pence each, of course. The great cathedral must pay for its upkeep, I suppose. Let's first view the nave. The next service isn't for another two hours, so we have plenty of time."

He never doubted the ladies would agree to his proposal and, indeed, they could not object, for he had something of the gamboling puppy in his demeanor, so keen was he to explore one of London's most worthy monuments.

"I've brought you a gift of sorts," he said, handing Anne a reddish root about a hand's width in size and lumpily misshapen in the middle, its body marked by several short, spindly protuberances.

"Whatever is it? It looks like a yam." Anne turned it over. "Did you dig this out of my uncle's garden? I did not know yams could be grown in London."

"I don't know what it is, but I found it in Hyde Park yesterday when I joined Mr. Darcy and Richard for a ride there. The gardeners were trimming bushes near the footpath and had cast this exceptional piece onto a pile of debris. I thought you might like to draw it. It's been cleaned and dried."

"Thank you, I think. It will prove a challenge to capture its likeness on paper." She stuffed the bulbous root into her reticule. "How is Miss Derrythorpe? Has she recovered herself?"

"She suffered a nervous headache most of the evening after viewing the lions and retired to bed early on Dr. Hamilton's advice. Yesterday she slept late and laid about the drawing room all morning, demanding biscuits and pots of tea and driving everyone to distraction. She would have joined us on our tour of the cathedral, except aunt Fitzwilliam wished to cosset her for another day."

They were interrupted by the arrival of a young woman, whom Miss Waygood rushed to introduce.

"Please allow me to make known to you my younger sister Mary." To Anne she said, "Mary and her husband, Will Kemble—no relation, so far as we know, to the famous acting and theatre managing family—live only a few blocks from here. I did not think you would object to her accompanying us on our tour today. We have few opportunities to visit with each other."

Anne welcomed Mrs. Kemble and the newly formed group followed Mr. Derrythorpe around to the north portico, where they passed under a small dome held aloft by great Corinthian columns. He knocked on the door, paid their entry fee, and led the ladies into the cathedral's cool transept. A gaunt, white-haired man approached with quiet dignity and offered to show the young persons the nave for two pence.

Miss Waygood and her sister chose to remain in the transept while Mr. Derrythorpe and Anne trailed after their imposing host. They crossed the black-and-white marbled floor, stared at Sir James Thornhill's painted domed ceiling soaring over-head, and each privately thought the nave plain and dreary. They listened while their guide described the three porticos and the two statues and the cost to the British people of build-ing the edifice. Mr. Derrythorpe was much enthralled by the spread-winged eagle that adorned the reader's desk, the whole surrounded by brass and gilt rails.

Anne's eye happened to be drawn to the transept, where she caught a scene being enacted in the dim light: Miss Waygood gripped Mrs. Kemble's arm, leaned toward her sister with a show of menace, and then exited the cathedral with great energy, giving a nod to the doorman. Mrs. Kemble smiled weakly when she spied Anne looking in her direction.

"Where has Miss Waygood gone?" asked Anne on their return.

"She has run an errand and suggested we continue our tour." Mrs. Kemble curtsied like a servant.

Readily adapting to their new circumstances, the trio moved on, climbing some two hundred and fifty steps to the whisper-ing gallery. Here they paused to catch their breath, admire the under-dome, and watch a few tourists milling about on the floor below. A family with children ranged themselves along the sides of the gallery, the four boys requiring considerable command to prevent them from running and yelling.

"I fear it's too crowded to try whispering," said a disappointed Mr. Derrythorpe. "Are you fit enough to keep climbing?" To Anne's hearty assent, he said with admiration, "You are game for anything. And you, Mrs. Kemble? Do you care to continue?"

Anne thought Mrs. Kemble's look suggested a preference to forego any additional exertion, but the three continued climbing the more than one hundred steps to the stone gallery. Here the passage was narrow, the shallow steps curving tightly like thread wound around a finger.

"I shouldn't like to meet up with anyone coming down the steps," said a breathless Anne.

When they passed a tiny alcove, Mrs. Kemble claimed to be bored with climbing and chose to rest on the niche's stone bench to wait for them.

Anne and Mr. Derrythorpe continued climbing, passing several more alcoves before emerging onto the outdoor gallery atop the colonnade. Although the wind was sharp, they walked the circumference and appreciated every view from the cathedral's vantage point atop Ludgate Hill. On the south side, they stood at the balustrade and marveled at the wherries plying London's river road and watched the vehicles and pedestrians maneuvering down the street.

"Look, is that not Miss Waygood there in front of the coach stand?" Mr. Derrythorpe nodded to the east.

Anne was forced to squint against the wind as her eyes scanned the crowd. She spied her governess talking to a well-dressed gentleman who stood with his back to the immense cathedral. Miss Waygood's face was hidden by the brim of her bonnet, but even from the top of St. Paul's Anne perceived the couple's familiarity.

"That is she, is it not? —The lady wearing the blue pelisse and bonnet. Who is that with her? Do you know him?"

"I am a little acquainted with him," replied Anne, feeling strangely betrayed by her governess's exceptional behavior. So this was why Mrs. Kemble had been invited to join their expedition. She served as chaperon while her older sister undertook a secret assignation. Of course, it might be an innocent encounter, but Anne was prepared to think otherwise and wondered what sort of mischief was afoot.

"You think them romantically involved?"

Anne nodded, her eyes scrutinizing her governess.

"I detect your disapproval. Do you not like him?"

"I believe him to be a kind and decent man, although I do not know him well." Stepping back from the railing, she asked, "Shall we continue?"

"Climbing to the gallery at the foot of the lantern will be a true test of our determination. I hope you aren't faint-hearted," teased Mr. Derrythorpe, "for it is only another one hundred and fifty steps to the top."

"Lead on," said Anne, smiling.

After fifty or sixty steps, they paused to catch their breath in the murky light. Mr. Derrythorpe spoke to the shadows: "You must not worry about Miss Waygood. She is a grown woman and knows her own mind."

Anne listened to the sounds of laughter echoing down the stairwell from the higher reaches. "What you say is true. She is always confident in herself. Indeed, I have often wished to possess the same degree of assurance, the same belief that I control my destiny. But what price can be placed on such freedom? If she and the gentleman choose to act in their own interests, may they deeply wound their families and friends? Which carries the greater cost: to harm your relations or to harm oneself?"

"An excellent question, but one I am not qualified to answer. I suspect we must weigh the cost on each side before deciding what to think. At least, that is what any rational person would do. Do you believe she may act irrationally?"

"I fear she may be contemplating it. I am afraid for them, for I believe his parents will not approve the match, but it seems to me that sometimes we cannot help ourselves. We pursue a person or object against our better judgment. I do not know why that is."

"We are the brightest species in God's firmament and can conquer our meaner impulses if we but apply ourselves—or so I've been taught."

Anne studied his youthful face. "You believe it so? Do you not think sometimes that we cannot help who we are? That we cannot repulse that which we desire? If we could control our animal instincts and worst natures then the posting houses and taverns would sell far less spirits than they do now. There would be less crime, less vice, less unhappiness in the world."

"Perhaps some vices bring happiness," Mr. Derrythorpe said jokingly.

"I fear you might be right."

"Besides, not many of us act rationally where matters of the heart are concerned," said Mr. Derrythorpe, not knowing how to respond to her thoughtful demeanor. "My sister is the perfect case. She is forever throwing herself at first one gentleman and then another. She falls in love at the drop of a glove and pleads with our parents for permission to marry Mr. Abbott or Mr. Castle or Mr. Newcome. She knows my parents will not support her schemes. Indeed, how could they? My sister's suitors never approach my parents for permission to address her, as is the proper thing to do. She has compromised herself in more than one case. Indeed, that is the true reason we were sent to London. Never mind measles, which our mother is perfectly able to manage. My immodest sister was found alone with a neighbor's son behind the barn, acting for all the world like a country harlot. Behind the barn!" Disgust rode his voice. "She's a goose and a terrible trial for my parents."

He proceeded upward a step or two before saying, "Give me your hand. The staircase is narrow and dark, and I shouldn't like you to lose your footing. The last thing we need is a sprained or broken ankle."

Anne obliged him as they continued upward. "You mustn't fret. Your sister is very young."

"She's much the same age as you, and I haven't seen you dangling after every gentleman you meet."

"It isn't because I don't wish to. Rather, I have little opportunity for meeting eligible men in Hunsford, which is only a village with few marital prospects and none my parents would consider appropriate."

Anne could not speak of her engagement to Fitzwilliam, for she was pained by a future narrowed to a single choice. She would be given no opportunity to choose a husband for herself. With good fortune Miss Derrythorpe might have a different fate.

"Your sister is pretty and sweet and good tempered. It is no wonder she enjoys a host of suitors, and the fault is not all on her side, you know."

"Perhaps not, but she could dampen her admirers' ardor if she chose to." They paused, releasing their handhold. Neither of them spoke for several minutes.

"Forgive me, but I was told that you are engaged to Mr. Darcy. Have I misunderstood?"

"No. I only recently learned of our engagement and am coming to terms with the idea."

Mr. Derrythorpe seemed satisfied with her reply and turned up the steps. Farther along they stopped to rest.

"Mr. Darcy is a decent sort. He doesn't treat me like a child, which Mr.—, well, which some other men do, and he asks my opinion now and then, as if he is truly interested in my ideas."

"Do you have many opinions?" asked Anne, helping herself to a bit of teasing.

"Oh, yes! I don't lack for them, although Mr. Darcy told me last week that I might expect to change a few of them in the coming year or two. I daresay he knows what he's talking about. He's quite intelligent, isn't he?"

"He is, indeed," Anne murmured.

"Your parents have chosen well, I think."

"True. I must consider myself fortunate."

Mr. Derrythorpe looked at her askance. "Are you against the idea of marriage?"

Anne startled at his tone. "Not at all. Why should you think so?"

"I am no great reader of character, but you seem to disapprove of Miss Waygood's desire to marry and also dislike the idea of marrying Mr. Darcy."

She thought him a very able reader, but said, "I'm not against marriage. It is only that despite Mr. Darcy being my cousin, I do not know him well. It is a daunting task to undertake this very intimate relationship when I have no idea what pleases him, what he values, what he hopes and strives for. I have much to learn and no clear way of learning it."

"All good points, but I think you worry overly. Marriage is a partnership. He will teach you what you need to know," said Mr. Derrythorpe as he pushed through the doors to the upper gallery.

They did not tarry long there, for a brisk breeze whipped the strings on Anne's bonnet and forced Mr. Derrythorpe to remove his hat. As they stood together watching the swirl of humans below, he said, "The pocket-guide speaks true. The pedestrians look like ants scurrying hither and yon in pursuit of some fairy-ground. It's thrilling to be part of it, don't you think?"

"It is certainly different from the peace and quiet of Rosings," said Anne as she took his arm to retreat from the wind.

There being no sign of Mrs. Kemble in the staircase, they continued circling downward until they reached the whispering gallery. Only one other couple stood on the opposite side of the dome, which spurred Mr. Derrythorpe to action.

"Wait here. I shall go around to the other side and speak to you. I have been told you must lay your head against the wall to hear me."

"My head? Surely you are joking."

He grinned. "Aye, place your ear against the stone."

Anne sat on the stone bench and watched him move nimbly along the narrow passage. He took a seat nearly directly opposite, smiling like a ten-year-old, and turned his head to speak. Anne pressed her ear to the stone.

"Can you hear me?"

"Yes! How strange."

"It's a marvel, isn't it? What an odd feature to find in a cathedral. Do you like it?"

"Very much, although I wonder how it works."

"I hope you won't look to me for answers, for I don't have any."

Anne laughed.

When they descended to the north transept they found themselves without chaperons but did not allow the fact to alter their plan.

They paid four pence to obtain access to the staircase that led to the curiosities, which included the library, the Geometrical Staircase, and Wren's model of the cathedral, all wonders to behold.

Their chaperons waited for them at the entrance. Miss Waygood held a package tucked under one arm and did not comment on her absence. "What do you care to see next?" she asked her charges, as though she had only stepped across the street to retrieve an order of new gloves. Mr. Derrythorpe was all for paying to see the Great Bell and the Clock-work, and so the group—restored to unity and conformity—set off in the direction of the southern tower. Mrs. Kemble looked as though she preferred to return to her housekeeping duties.

Chapter 15

A Shared Secret

Anne spent the next morning cheerfully anticipating the drive in Hyde Park, having first learned of the excursion at the breakfast table when her mother received a letter from her sister agreeing to the plan. On hearing that Mr. Wickham would be included in the outing, Anne's heartbeat quickened.

From that point on nothing her mother or her governess said perturbed her joyful spirit. Indeed, Miss Waygood noticed. "You look like the cat that has lapped up the cook's cream. What are you so excited about?"

"We are joining the Darcys for a drive in Hyde Park. It is a fine day for it, I think." Anne wanted to ask about Miss Waygood's unexplained errand but feared she would be scolded for it. In the four years her governess had lived at Rosings, Anne could not recall an instance in which she had ever suspected Isabelle of duplicity. Her governess had always upheld the virtues of honesty and openness, reminding Anne often of their importance in leading a happy life. This sneaking about and seemingly lying to—or, at least, misleading—her was out of character. "What shall you do while we are gone?"

Miss Waygood peered at Anne over the top of her glasses. "I shall visit my sister's family and determine whether Mary's view of St. Paul's matches yours."

"If it's a rapt description you seek," said Anne, "you had best speak with Mr. Derrythorpe."

"I might do so if I had an hour to spare for his raptures."

They parted to dress for their outings, and Anne now sat opposite Mr. Wickham in the Darcy carriage. Her parents and uncle and aunt were in the second carriage. Everybody was in good humor. A lingering fog had mostly burned off, giving way to a hazy and not particularly warm day. The carriages wound their way through Mayfair and entered the carriage road from the southeast corner of Hyde Park. Georgiana, sitting next to Anne, exclaimed at every stylish hat, parasol, and elegant equipage, while Fitzwilliam, sitting opposite, gave the occasional nod or modest wave to an acquaintance on foot or horseback. Mr. Wickham sat in perfect ease, a wool muffler thrown around his neck.

"Is that Sir Robert?" asked a gleeful Georgiana, pointing across the lawn to a stout gentleman with a bonny lady on his arm.

"It isn't polite to point," said Fitzwilliam, swiveling to look over his shoulder and across the lawn. "Yes, I believe it is." He caught Georgiana's wounded look and knew he had spoken over-harshly. She was only nine years old and excited to be taking a drive in the park. He smiled and took her hand. "Shall we go speak with him?"

"Yes, please," the girl whispered.

"Stop the coach," called Fitzwilliam. He assisted his sister down from the carriage. "Drive on," he told the coachman. "We will catch you in a few minutes." Taking Georgiana's hand, he sauntered off across the beaten grass and called a greeting to his friend.

"Do you know him?" Anne asked Mr. Wickham as the carriage jerked forward.

"He is Sir Robert Alfriston-Seal, third baronet and a member of the House of Commons. Sir Robert's property lies some fifteen miles north of Pemberley. Fitz is attracted to the man's military zeal, for Sir Robert supports the wars against Napoleon and France. When they are together there is much talk of battles and skirmishes and intelligence published in *The Gentleman's Magazine*. Poor Sir Robert. He has been in the doldrums since Pitt fell out of favor but holds to the belief that his favorite will lead the country again. Sir Robert is a true optimist."

"I had not realized you were so acquainted with the local families in Derbyshire. Indeed, I cannot recall hearing you speak of your country friends."

"Sir Robert has a son only a year younger than I. We often find occasions to enjoy each other's company."

Judging Mr. Wickham's grin, Anne said, "Perhaps starting trouble is more the case."

"What else is there to do in the country? A man must find amusements where he may." Wickham's coy smile was designed to steer her thinking in another direction, for what he most wished to avoid was being asked questions about his activities in Derbyshire or London. "You seem bent on making trouble yourself. Do not pretend you don't understand me. After observing your choice of reading material in your uncle's library, I believe you plan to become a surgeon. Where do you intend to study? Edinburgh, perhaps?"

Anne caught her breath, suddenly conscious of the damage Mr. Wickham could do if he reported her clandestine activity. She sought the safest course by making light of his teasing. "I am considering Edinburgh, but I may train with an apothecary and afterward study medicine at St. George's here in London."

She wished to sound saucy and teasing but feared her demeanor betrayed her uncertainty.

Wickham took up her joke. "That is a good strategy and will ensure your success, should you be accepted as a pupil at university, which seems doubtful. Still, you might find a patron to underwrite your studies, after which you will astonish everybody who thinks the daughter of a baronet—indeed, the granddaughter of an earl—cannot train as a surgeon or physician. You clearly have the aptitude and discipline for study, but one aspect of our little *tête-à-tête* in the library puzzles me. Why were you disturbed on seeing my humorous print after studying Hunter's engravings of dead infants?"

Anne's cheeks sported two spots of red, for she did not like the turn of this conversation and knew not how to guard against his provoking intimacy.

Fearing he had pushed her too far, Wickham said, "Very well, I shall not tease you but instead offer brotherly advice: take care her ladyship does not learn of your study. Lady Catherine has particular ideas on what constitutes proper behavior for a young lady and would make your life a misery if she were to learn that you were studying medical books. Do not fret. I shall never betray you to your mother or to anyone in the Darcy family. Indeed, I can think of no one with whom I care to share this information. It will be our secret. We are friends, after all, are we not? And friends take care of one another." His reassuring smile seemed to satisfy her. "Are you excited about your family's dinner party? Sir Lewis invited me to attend, along with the Darcys, of course."

Anne's trust was restored by his promise and kindly smile. "Oh, yes, for we are expecting a large group of friends and family. Mama and I shall review the menu tomorrow. Miss Waygood shall play for us and there will be dancing. The Fitzwilliams will be there, along with Miss and Mr.

Derrythorpe, and our Kentish neighbors, the Ormistons and the Dighursts, whom you have not met. They are all merry, Mr. Ormiston in particular. I look forward to it."

"Excellent! We shall have some fun. But I warn you: I expect to stand up with you twice during the evening." A thought struck him. "Will your engagement to Fitz be announced?"

"You know of it?"

"Of course. How could I not? Fitz has known of it for several years, and I daresay even Georgiana has been told. Surely this is a source of joy for your families, both being now relieved of any worry over finding a suitable match for the two of you. I must say, the idea of wedding your cousin seems to agree with you, for you are blooming like a summer flower this morning."

"I wish—I am not sure quite how I feel about it. It is all so sudden."

"It will settle on you soon enough, and then you will not be seized with perilous imaginings."

"Do you think so? I fear marriage might hold as many terrors as the meaner alleys of London. A bride must learn her husband's whims and foibles, his pleasures and desires …" A blush overwhelmed her, for while she was thinking of housekeeping, she suspected Mr. Wickham was not. "A husband must do the same, of course. It is rather overwhelming."

"Ah, dear cousin, you make me smile."

Wickham found her innocence amusing. Being shy and properly modest, she would feel unnerved by thoughts of her wedding night and the expectations Fitzwilliam might have of her. This was only to be expected. In time, she would lose her fears and inhibitions. In fact, she might come to enjoy the intimate aspects of married life. Many women did. But if she was not so lucky, a secret adventure might prove enticing. Provided the principals were discreet, a married woman could take a lover. This was especially true if she had produced the expected heir, and her husband was willing to turn a blind eye to her love affair. So much depended on timing and circumstances.

Oh, the stories he could tell about Fitzwilliam, if he were so inclined, but this he would never do, for he had more to risk from exposure than the ever-prudent Fitz.

Not wanting to make her nervous or uneasy, he said, "Are you looking forward to Sir Robert's ball? I believe your family has been sent an invitation."

"Yes, the invitation arrived yesterday."

"You will enjoy meeting Sir Robert," said Wickham with a nod toward the gentleman, who was taking leave of Fitzwilliam and Georgiana, "and his eldest son, Alfrit, as he is known by nearly everybody. It will be a lavish affair, for Sir Robert never spares an expense when entertaining. Would that not suit you?"

Anne nodded in agreement as Georgiana came running toward the carriage. The coachman brought the rig to a sudden stop.

"Sir Robert promises to let me ride his new pony when we return to Pemberley," she said, nearly breathless with excitement.

"Then you are fortunate, indeed," said Anne, helping the child into the carriage.

Fitzwilliam climbed in after his sister and settled on the bench. He tossed a complacent smile at Anne, which astonished her no end.

Chapter 16

Heavy Swells

Lady Catherine could be heard issuing orders to the staff in a loud, imperious voice. The French chef, Monsieur Jacques Fontaine, who was new to Chidham House, exclaimed, "*Oui, oui, Madame. Il en sera ainsi.* It will be so." In his excitement, he rattled in French, nearly forgetting his English.

Chidham House was being readied for a dinner party, a continuation of the tradition begun several years previously, in which the de Bourghs hosted their relations, the Darcys of Derbyshire and the Fitzwilliams of Wiltshire, one evening in early December. New at table this season were their Kentish neighbors, the Dighursts, who leased Bardolph Hall, and the Ormistons, whose smallish park of one hundred acres—named Holcombe Manor in honor of its valley pastures—was situated a mere two miles from Rosings Park, the de Bourgh's country seat of nearly three hundred acres.

The properties all enjoyed a neighborly proximity to the village of Hunsford, which claimed no special recognition of service or commerce, other than being on the road that progressed in an easterly direction toward Tunbridge through

Kent's fine rolling hills and farmland before branching north to Maidstone and southerly to the coast.

As Anne refilled her teacup, Lady Catherine paused in the doorway. "It is time to review the preparations for this evening's dinner," said she, before resuming her march upstairs to the morning room, the breathless chef scurrying behind her.

Anne laid down her bread, recognizing a summons when she heard one. She hurried down her tea before rising to follow her mother.

If a room can be said to serve as the heart of a house, the morning room at Chidham was such a room. Situated at the front of the house, its warmth was derived partly from the morning light filtered through the curtained windows and partly from a small, efficient fireplace whose cast-iron grate burned coal fiercely for several hours. To either side of the fireplace, tall built-in cupboards with glazed window panels displayed vases, tea canisters, and platters of mostly blue and white china that matched the marble tiles lining the fire surround. Although not large, the morning room was perfectly proportioned, being sufficiently spacious to accommodate Lady Catherine's mahogany *table à écrire*, Anne's small but serviceable writing table, and two plush armchairs.

One might think the armchairs stood ready to receive the weary body of any staff member called to give Lady Catherine an accounting, but one would be mistaken in the idea, as the chef was discovering.

Anne entered to find her mother seated at her writing table, her ink pot and quills ready. Mrs. Juggins, the housekeeper, stood to one side, her arms crossed over her ample belly; she studied the French chef with a wary eye, not liking the idea of relinquishing her duties to a foreigner or, indeed, to anybody else. The candles in the central chandelier and gilded girandoles had been lit, their flames giving light and comfort.

Monsieur Fontaine, perhaps feeling his ease in the warm, cheerful room, seated himself with a flourish in one of the armchairs facing his employer. Predictably, Lady Catherine froze, one hand holding the newly revised menu and the other poised atop her household account book. Her withering eye never left the chef's face. Monsieur Fontaine, whose manner bespoke his abiding belief in the superiority of the French over every other species on the planet, and most especially the English, blinked in confusion and then rose slowly to his feet, a dawning comprehension lighting his countenance. After adjusting his starched jacket, he glowered and clasped his hands behind his back.

The man was a quick study, for he remained standing, his legs braced for heavy swells.

Anne took the chair at her writing table, curious to see how the chef would handle himself during the coming interview.

Lady Catherine opened with a demand.

"Why does the menu not include pheasant? It was requested specifically for this function—Sir Lewis dearly loves pheasant." After this volley, she progressed to a detailed inquisition regarding the chef's choice of sauces, glazes, sides, and desserts.

Monsieur Fontaine defended every decision. He argued for beef bouillon instead of a cassoulet; explained that Carlton House had garnered every pheasant within a hundred miles of London—even White's had no pheasants; offered assurance that her guests would be delighted with Salmis of Quails, the recipe being favored by the Prince of Wales himself and much heralded on the continent; and praised the selected wines with affection, which showed he was truly French.

Even though he was sweaty and red-faced by the time he left, Anne believed he had held his own against her mother, although below-stairs he might find himself bested by the housekeeper. Her guineas were on Mrs. Juggins.

"Bah. The French!" said Lady Catherine after he decamped for the kitchen. "I would not court them for all the King's coin. Why Mrs. Ormiston employs a French chef at Holcombe surpasses all understanding."

As the morning progressed, Anne's energy flagged. Her spirits were low, which fact she attributed to the news of Miss Waygood's impending departure and the lengthy protocol for interviewing the housekeeper regarding the service of silver, plate, glassware, linens, and other accessories to be used over the course of the evening. The one bright star in her firmament was the assurance that Mr. Wickham would attend.

Chapter 17

Animal Spirits

The Chidham House footmen swarmed to relieve the Darcys and Mr. Wickham of their coats, gloves, and hats, after which Juggins escorted them to the first-story drawing room.

"Welcome, welcome!" cried Sir Lewis as he passed each guest along to Lady Catherine and Anne standing at his side. "I hope your travel this evening was not too onerous."

Everyone exclaimed at the cold, expressed fears of heavy rain overnight, and offered well-wishes to their hosts.

Anne curtsied to aunt Darcy, who kissed her cheek and exclaimed, "How pretty you look this evening, niece." Uncle Darcy presented his cheek for a kiss, while Fitzwilliam shook her hand, his form correct as always, his face expressing neither delight nor dismay in seeing her. Mr. Wickham next grasped her hand, giving her a sly wink before saying, "I have never seen you look so charming and hope you have not forgotten your promise to dance with me." He pressed his lips against her fingers, the touch soft as velvet.

No one spied his impertinent behavior, for the Ormistons had entered the room, their cheeks brushed red from the raw

December wind. Mr. Godfrey Ormiston, the second son of the 2nd Baron Metcalfe, was a handsome, barrel-chested man whose loud and hearty laugh and love of hunting and fishing made him a favorite among the local Kentish gentry.

He and Sir Lewis had taken to each other on first being introduced, forging a bond built on their mutual interest in new agricultural methods for land improvement. Mrs. Ormiston's love of parties and suppers endeared her to all of Hunsford and half the county, which Anne suspected annoyed Lady Catherine no end.

Catching Anne's hand, Mr. Ormiston said, "You look well this evening. Are you enjoying Town?"

"Very much so, sir. And you?"

He shook his head in a mock display of despair. "I might enjoy Town and its delights if only my ladies would buy fewer hats and gloves and silks. They are emptying London of its finery." He grinned at his wife.

"Mr. Ormiston, do behave," said Mrs. Ormiston. "Surely you want your daughter and me to be better dressed than your cows and sheep."

"Please allow me think on it, ma'am," he replied, giving his wife an exaggerated bow.

Anne joined the laughter but observed that her mother withheld a disapproving comment.

In her ladyship's opinion, their banter was not proper, even among close neighbors.

Everyone else, however, enjoyed the joke, including the Ormistons' only daughter, Clarinda, who looked very stylish in her pale green silk gown and white lacy shawl, and her two older brothers—Charles, the first son and presumptive heir, and Lawrence, their second and favorite son. The Ormiston children—all six of them, including the younger boys who did not accompany their parents this evening—were exceedingly handsome, favoring their father in having robust personalities and crowns of curly blonde hair.

No sooner had Sir Lewis introduced the Ormistons to the Darcys than the Dighursts, the Fitzwilliams, and the Derrythorpes arrived, stirring a new round of introductions.

Anne greeted her family and neighbors, happy to see so many smiling, familiar faces. To Miss Derrythorpe she said, "Are you are sufficiently recovered from our adventure with the Tower lions to play the pianoforte this evening?"

Sir Lewis was thinking along the same lines. "I hope you brought your supple fingers to play for us," he said, wiggling his fingers, "for we all look forward to a simple musical program and dancing after dinner."

Everyone was in good looks and more than ready for a hot repast. When dinner was announced, the happy guests entered the dining room. Miss Ormiston approached Anne hurriedly, whispering, "La! Miss Derrythorpe is a natural beauty, is she not? Who would have thought a mean village like Clun could produce a child possessing such sweet features. She will conquer a few hearts when she has acquired a little Town bronze, but her sort of beauty never lasts."

Anne recognized Miss Ormiston's resentment at not being the brightest ornament in the room. That honor belonged to Miss Derrythorpe, who exclaimed at the table's loveliness and in doing so revealed how little Town polish she possessed.

It was difficult to fault the newcomer, however, for much work had gone toward preparing the dinner. Dozens of tall candles graced the mantel and side tables, each throwing a cheerful glow against the red damask walls. Two crystal chandeliers hung over the table, their candle flames dazzling against the white coffered ceiling. Along the length of the table, fragrant branches of evergreens and sprigs of holly and rosemary intertwined the silver candelabra and stands of glazed fruit.

Sir Lewis anchored the table's head, while Lady Catherine sat regally at the bottom end. On her signal the servants jumped to lay the first course and the sounds of clinking dinnerware and laughter filled the room.

Anne relished the convivial atmosphere. As one dinner course followed another and the warmth of the room increased, she joked with her cousin Richard, teased Mr. Derrythorpe, and drank more wine than was her habit. She listened to Fitzwilliam and Charles debating Bonaparte's strategies with Mr. Dighurst, while Mrs. Dighurst looked on her son with great complacency. She heard Major Dighurst inquire whether the young and estimable Lieutenant Derrythorpe of the __th Regiment of Foot was any relation of Miss and Mr. Derrythorpe, only to learn of there being no known connection. The warm looks she received from Mr. Wickham stirred her heartstrings more than wine could ever do.

Their repast finished, the guests rose to return to the drawing room for music and dancing. Although there was no set musical program, the young ladies were each expected to perform. Miss Ormiston was invited to play the pianoforte first, which charge she accepted with enthusiasm, for she had recently memorized a rondo. Her fingers upon the keys were not nearly so nimble as those of Miss Derrythorpe, who played a vigorous Clementi sonatina and astonished everyone with her lively skill. Anne next took the stool and played "Greensleeves," a simple melody that pleased every expectant ear. She, in turn, relinquished her place to Miss Waygood, who had joined the party after dinner at Sir Lewis's invitation.

Anne smiled and nodded her thanks as she returned to her seat, feeling mortified to play so stupidly after Miss Derrythorpe's vivid performance. Would that she could have declined to play, but as it was expected of her, she had no choice but to embarrass herself.

Lady Anne joined her. "Your performance has improved since last I heard you."

"You are very kind. I have been practicing, but I lack the dexterity to play well. Miss Derrythorpe and Miss Waygood are the true musicians."

"Yes, they are passionate, which is a requisite for great art. Although few can claim a natural passion, regular practice and a determination to understand the music can lend emotion to one's performance. If you continue to apply yourself, you will be rewarded."

"Then I will practice more to please you."

Lady Anne nodded her approval. "Would that Miss Ormiston disciplined herself. She has remarkable assurance for one so young but lacks spirit."

Anne thought her aunt had the right of it: Miss Ormiston plays with confidence but no feeling, whereas I play with feeling but no confidence. Their different styles made her wonder whether passion could be acquired through training, a feat she rather doubted.

When Miss Waygood offered to play again, Sir Lewis called for dancing.

"Anne, my own sweet girl," he said, his eyes refulgent with affection and pride, "we must open the dance. We are not a large party but shall have some fun."

Anne took his hand. "Will you allow me to stand on your feet, as you did when I was a child?"

Sir Lewis laughed.

"I fear my arches are not so sturdy as they used to be, but well I remember how we swayed in time to the music when you were a wee girl and stood on my shoes."

Dancing was Anne's gift. Where the uninformed observer expected awkwardness and shyness, they discovered her natural rhythm and joy of movement. She was graceful and revealed no artifice or self-consciousness. In this one area, Anne won her mother's approval.

When the dance finished, Sir Lewis called for a change of partners, there being no need for formality in their intimate setting.

Anne first partnered Mr. Derrythorpe, after which she stood up with Fitzwilliam. In true form, she felt awkward dancing with her cousin and feared she could not engage him in any worthy conversation. It did not matter, for Fitzwilliam focused on the dance pattern and made little eye contact with her. As they paired and parted, Anne became less concerned with earning his good opinion and more engrossed in the music and movement.

She caught her mother's satisfied smile as the dance ended, at which point Mr. Wickham gained her hand.

Anne felt a frisson of excitement as she placed her hand in his. When the music ended, he drew her a little to one side. "You are by far the prettiest lady in the room. I should enjoy a few minutes alone with you. Do you have the nerve to meet me in the library? No one will interrupt us there."

Anne glanced from the pianoforte to the chairs ranged against one wall, fearing someone—her Papa or aunt Darcy or Miss Ormiston—might be observing them, but no one paid any attention. The murmur of the dancers seeking new partners reverberated around the room, while Miss Waygood received suggestions for the next musical offering.

"If you fear being detected, we shall tell a simple story: you are seeking a book for me. It would be natural for you to offer." Wickham bowed to her and stepped away.

Anne felt a stab of panic as she watched him thread his way through the dancers. He was a handsome man—tall and broad-shouldered, with a boyish face and impish grin, all attributes she found beguiling.

Should she follow him? She wished to know what he would say to her, but her heart pounded in her chest like a wooden mallet on a drum. A furtive glance about the room spurred her courage. She reached a decision and stepped into the hall. Ignoring the two footmen on the landing, she crossed to the stairs and began a sedate descent. Her calmness of temper was all for show, for her heart seemed fit to burst else Juggins catch her. *That hardly seems likely,* she reminded herself, for the servants take the backstairs and are busy laying tea.

On the ground story the library doorway was mostly dark, the staff having snuffed the candles after the guests went upstairs to the drawing rooms. She paused to steady her breathing in the faint light of the hall's girandole candles before touching the door with a trembling hand. A warm hand took her arm and pulled her into the shadow.

"Cousin Anne, I feared you might lose your courage. I should have known better, for you are a determined little thing." Wickham lifted her chin. "Shall I kiss you?"

Anne's heart beat so wildly that she could not speak.

"Yes, I think I should."

His kiss was proper and discreet. His voice caressed. His gentle manner reassured.

"Come," he said, drawing her to the sofa in the shadows. He sat down and pulled her onto the cushion beside him. She giggled nervously.

"Do I make you laugh?" he asked, rubbing her hand.

"Sometimes you do, and other times you seem determined to either annoy or distract me." In the dim light she caught the smile in his eyes.

"I like the idea of distracting you." Cupping her face in his hands, he kissed first one cheek, then the other. "Your skin smells sweet," he murmured. Finding no fear or dismay in her look, he kissed her lips, this time with more warmth.

Anne was nearly breathless. With each velvet touch she felt light as air shimmering on a hot summer's day. When she raised her arms to encircle his neck, he deftly pulled her closer to him, saying, "Will you let down your hair?"

"I dare not," she whispered, surprised to find a fragment of common sense, "else I fail to fix it properly before returning upstairs."

"You need not worry," he said, removing the ribbon that encircled the braided knot atop her head. "I shall serve as your personal hair-dresser." Next he tugged on the hair pin and arranged the long braid over her shoulder. He squeezed her small breast.

The agreeable sensation set Anne afire. When his kisses became more ardent, she did not flinch but stoked his lust with hers.

"Anne!"

Sir Lewis and Fitzwilliam stood in the doorway.

Anne pushed against Mr. Wickham's chest and scrambled awkwardly to her feet. Mr. Wickham rose as well, a vacuous stare on his face.

"Papa—"

"Hush. Fitzwilliam, escort this rogue upstairs, please."

Mr. Wickham, momentarily perturbed at being discovered, pulled at his coat sleeves, ignored his host's frowning countenance, and pushed past Fitzwilliam blocking the doorway.

Sir Lewis closed the door, moved to the desk, and took his time lighting an oil lamp. He studied his daughter. "I never thought to find you in such a situation. Did I not warn you about Mr. Wickham?"

"Yes, Papa," said a subdued Anne.

"How is it that I find you alone with him?"

Anne could not answer. She wiped a tear away with a trembling hand.

"Take this," he said, handing her his handkerchief. "I understand your animal spirits, Anne. They are natural and good when enjoyed within the confines of marriage, but not in this willful manner. You cannot realize how small a thing can damage your reputation. I had not believed you as wanton as this. Indeed, I never expected you to behave with so little regard for yourself under any circumstances, much less with guests in the house. Only imagine what Fitzwilliam must think. His engagement to you is known to the family and a few close friends, which gives him certain expectations regarding your behavior, among them being the right to expect you to behave with decorum and dignity, especially when in company. For him to find you in so daring and indelicate a situation must alter his opinion of you, and not for the better."

Anne sniffled.

"Stop crying. It does no good," he said with vigor. "I will send Dobbie up to rearrange your hair. When you return to the drawing room, you will behave as any proper young lady should do. But think on this: all you have, Anne—all you will ever have in this world—is your reputation. It deserves guarding." He frowned down on her. "We shall speak of this again."

When he left, Anne sobbed into his handkerchief. Her world might never be as it was before this night.

She felt sickened on realizing the true awfulness of her behavior. While she waited to be rescued, she dabbed the damp linen against her cheeks and marveled at how she came to be here. Common sense and noble virtues had deserted her completely, and with hardly a care she had abandoned a lifetime of natural goodness for a few furtive kisses.

Why, she had less sense than a giddy fledgling teetering on a limb, for she believed herself ready for the world. She had launched into the ether, trusted to intuition, and gave no thought to consequences. Would Papa no longer think of her as his beloved and dutiful daughter? Would she ever again be his own dear girl? Recalling the look on his face bruised her heart. She blew her nose and looked up to see her maid approach.

Dobbie's sad face told her much of what had been lost in this one fit of passion. No gentle comfort was offered. Dobbie was business-like and grim-faced as she fixed Anne's hair, after which she dropped a quick curtsy and left the library, never saying a word.

It took an iron will to climb the stairs to the drawing room, for Anne was not sure what she would find there. With each step she tried a different expression—brave, serious, vaguely pleasant—but none was a proper mask for the circumstances. Fortunately, no one seemed aware of the cataclysm that had occurred below; no one had twigged to her indiscretion. A cup of tea did little to steady her nerves, especially when she spied her father speaking with uncle Darcy.

Oh, how awful! Of course my uncle must be informed of the event, and my aunt, too, no doubt. What must they think of me after this evening?

Her eyes scanned the guests until she spied Mr. Wickham near the pianoforte, where he entertained Miss Ormiston. He loomed over her, his facial expression the very mark of respectful entreaty, and asked a question. Her reply brought forth a deep laugh. He ignored his dear cousin, as if the two of them had never been closeted in the library trading kisses.

At the other end of the room, Fitzwilliam stood in a clutch of uncles and guests, seemingly absorbed in their conversation. He had retreated to the safe, predictable domain of men. Standing with his back to the room, he ignored Mr. Wickham.

Anne took a chair against the wall, relieved to have a few minutes to gather her wits. While she considered her situation, her eyes came to rest on Miss Waygood and Mr. Dighurst. They appeared to be avoiding one another this evening, for the two of them had not shared more than a few words. Had they crossed swords over some trifle? Or were they trying to keep their emotions well regulated so as not to give a hint of their affection? Miss Waygood cradled a cup of punch in her hands. Mr. Dighurst rested one arm against the fireplace mantel, his wavy hair brushed back from his forehead, his fashionable attire revealing a powerful body and muscled shoulders.

There was something intimate in their attitudes.

As this thought occurred to her, Mr. Dighurst passed a note to Miss Waygood, who seemed momentarily flummoxed by his recklessness. She recovered quickly, however, and scanned the room to confirm their safety.

Her eyes locked on Anne's quizzical face.

Anne lowered her eyes and appeared absorbed in her tea. She wondered at their stealthy action but could not help thinking of her own.

Tomorrow might bring more than one reckoning.

Chapter 18

A Plump Pike

"I've brought hot chocolate for you," said Dobbie, setting a cup on Anne's bed-side table. She observed her charge's wan expression and did not mention the gossip below-stairs about the doings after last night's dinner. She was not surprised to learn from Sir Lewis about Miss Anne succumbing to the wicked ways of Mr. Wickham, for she knew he was unaccountably attractive to the gentler sex. True, she had not suspected Anne's regard for the rogue, but she had observed her aversion to Mr. Darcy, plain enough. It seemed manly looks and a flashy smile had trumped good character and pleasing manners. Well, strong measures would deal with this sort of foolishness. "You must get dressed, for it is going on one o'clock. You'll be needin' something to eat."

"I'm not hungry."

"You cannot lie abed all day, love. That will not do. You must get up. Shall you wear your green dotted muslin today?"

"If you like."

Dobbie was unaccustomed to such behavior as this. Miss Anne was seldom so lackadaisical. Her usual temper was to challenge and explore and ask questions and show a little gumption. At the moment she looked as though all her gumption had been squeezed right out, like a well-squashed lemon.

Mayhap that was a good thing, given last night's mischief.

A double knock penetrated the bedchamber door. Miss Waygood stuck her head in. "I thought to see how you do."

Dobbie gave the governess a knowing eye before leaving them to visit. Perhaps a few words from Miss Waygood would rouse Anne from the lethargy into which she had sunk and set her on a proper course.

Miss Waygood forced Anne to make room for her to sit on the edge of the bed. "What is to be done with you? Did I not tell you that Mr. Wickham was not to be trusted?"

Anne could not look her governess in the eye.

"Will you not defend yourself?" asked Miss Waygood.

"I cannot see that we did anything so very bad."

"Nothing so very bad? This is no time for joking. You snuck—I see that look—yes, *snuck* away from your friends and family and met privately with a young man of dubious reputation. You caused your relations no end of grief, for such an indiscretion cannot be kept secret, especially from the servants, whose tongues will wag at your expense. And worse, you embarrassed your father—and Mr. Darcy—when they discovered you half-undressed, I hear, in the library! Is this not bad behavior? I could hardly credit the stories I heard about you until I spoke with Sir Lewis."

"You spoke with Papa?"

"Yes. Your awful machination required us to consider what actions might be taken to mitigate the damage. You are fortunate that only family and close friends who care for your reputation were in attendance last night, else every newsmonger in London might feast on news of your recklessness. Your mother—you know her nature—is nearly hysterical and blames me for this episode. I will not, cannot, address with you the particulars of my discussion with Lady Catherine, who had plenty to say about how your upbringing has gone astray. She casts blame everywhere. Sadly, it is your father who grieves most over this situation. He would not allow me to take any responsibility for last night's incident and believes himself to be at fault. He thinks he has been too indulgent, too willing to give you rein to do as you wish. Had he been more faithful in his guardianship of you, he told me, you would not have been tempted by the likes of Mr. Wickham."

"But I love him, Isabelle. I've never known a kinder man, except Papa, of course. Mr. Wickham is all goodness toward me."

Anne had reached this conclusion after retiring to bed, where she lay awake recalling her clandestine meeting. Her feelings held fast, even after being discovered alone with him. True, she had behaved foolishly—recklessly, even—but felt no regret for receiving his affection. As was probably the case with most felons, she only regretted being caught.

"You love him? What do you know of love? How can you believe a man like Mr. Wickham is good-hearted? He has been flirting with you, toying with your affection, drawing you in, and when he saw an opportunity to be alone with you, he seized it. He hooked you like a plump pike and never mind your reputation. He cared nothing for it. *His* reputation won't suffer in the least. Women will find him as beguiling as ever, I daresay, even though he nearly seduced you, the daughter of a baronet, and practically under your father's nose."

Miss Waygood observed her charge's puffy red eyes and the mulish curve to her mouth.

"And this—this is the type of man to whom you would bind yourself?" she continued. "A proper young man, a man worthy of your love and trust, would think better of you. He would never place you in an awkward or compromising situation, as Mr. Wickham has done. Can you imagine Mr. Darcy inviting you or any other young lady to meet him secretly? The very idea is incredible, for he is aware of the harm such action can do. Mr. Darcy is too much a gentleman to risk harming a lady's reputation. I encourage you to think on these matters, dear one, for you have grown ignorant and willful this past year. A part of me can understand your attraction to Mr. Wickham, even though I cannot condone it, but to see you disrespect your father and embarrass your intended astonishes me." She let that comment sink in. "Sir Lewis shall speak with you after he meets with your uncle. Now, get dressed. I am instructed to take you for a walk in the park."

Anne thought it prudent not to mention her governess's own questionable behavior.

Chapter 19

A Bad Business

While Miss Waygood marshaled a distraught Anne through Kensington Gardens, Sir Lewis sampled a robust port in George Darcy's library.

A fire had been laid to ward off the chill of a dreary evening, and the gentlemen eased themselves into the two wing-backed chairs facing the fire's warmth. For a long while they were content to stare into the well-stoked blaze.

Mr. Darcy broke the silence. "This is a bad business. I never thought George so lost to all sense of propriety that he would impose himself on a member of our family."

"Have you spoken to him?" asked Sir Lewis.

"Yes, but I fear it did no good. How does one work on such a man? He has been brought up to the same standard as Fitzwilliam, but his character is completely different. Fitzwilliam would never be so reckless or impudent as to disregard the strictures and expectations of society, whereas George seems to delight in testing them. I suspect he is a rogue at heart, for he attracts ladies like nectar to a bee. There is no taming him, I fear."

Glancing at his fireside companion, Mr. Darcy wondered whether he should have been less forthright. Perhaps 'tis true: the better part of valor is discretion.

In truth, his namesake and godson had been troublesome from a young age.

There was the time a fourteen-year-old George Wickham had been caught kissing old Turchill's youngest daughter, who was a child herself. While the girl's father admired the new stallion in Mr. Darcy's barn, George had enticed the girl into the shrubbery near the drive. An awkward moment occurred when the couple was pulled from the bushes. The girl's ravaged lips, rosy as strawberries, suggested she had been a willing participant. Turchill had remained standoffish for months, even though his property was situated only four miles from Pemberley, and he had used to visit the Darcy family often. Afterwards he visited Pemberley rarely and always alone.

Numerous other incidents came to mind and appalled a godfather who was disposed to be kind and generous—up to a point. Had his godson intended to cross the traditional line of decorum and, if indeed he had, what was the proper way of dealing with the rebellion?

In fact, what sort of intervention could succeed in a young man of nineteen years? George was only six months younger than Fitzwilliam and would reach his majority in two years' time, after which there were no grounds for trying to influence or interfere with his behavior. At age one and twenty, George would be an adult and free to exercise all rights and responsibilities granted in law. He could marry without permission, buy and sell property, dispose of an estate, sign contracts, and otherwise manage his own affairs.

Feeling as though he stood in a quagmire Mr. Darcy retrieved the bottle of port, saying, "Would that George could acquire some of Fitzwilliam's natural reserve and dignity. I cannot help thinking how distressed his father would be if he were alive today."

"The elder Mr. Wickham has been dead, what, these past two years?" asked Sir Lewis, merely to be polite.

"Closer to three now, I believe," said Mr. Darcy, topping up his companion's glass.

The men each took the measure of the other and wondered how to keep the peace between them, for their mutual admiration had been steadfast over many years. In the early days of their marriages, they had been busy with the demands of their estates and their own business concerns and seldom had an opportunity for companionship, Derbyshire being no easy distance from Kent. Not until the children started to arrive did they discover a bond of civility and goodwill that eased them over several rough patches, including, between their families, one miscarriage and the deaths of three infants. They were loath now to test their friendship. Mr. Darcy knew Sir Lewis expected some sort of punishment for Wickham's behavior. Sir Lewis knew his friend and relation was struggling to find a just penalty for a godson he truly loved.

"I do not hold Anne responsible for this fiasco," said Mr. Darcy. "She is young and trusting, which is to her credit. Her attraction to George is understandable, if not excusable."

"I cannot agree with you there. Innocence is no protection. My mother used sometimes to say: 'It is a blind goose that knows not a fox from a fern bush.'" His brow bunched into neat folds as he swirled the port in his glass. "Anne, like Fitzwilliam, has been brought up to be mindful of duty, to respect her elders, to trust her parents' judgment, and to behave with decorum. She seems not to have learned some of these lessons, for which I hold myself responsible. I have been far too permissive. Indeed, I was negligent in not detecting her admiration for Mr. Wickham."

Mr. Darcy snorted. "Humph. You might sell your services as a seer if you could read any woman's heart or mind, and think of the income you would generate, for you'd have a steady supply of customers."

This comment made Sir Lewis smile. "Women are a mystery, I agree. How well can Shakespeare be said to have understood women?"

"Now there is a topic we might debate until the cows come home, but no good would come of the time spent discussing the point, however enjoyable the effort. In any event, your daughter—as dear to you as my own daughter is to me—knows little of the world's ugly ways, which is our preference."

"You are right. None the less, Anne worries me. I expected her to behave foolishly over some young man—who among us did not allow our animal spirits to get the better of us when we were children?—but I had not imagined she could do something so dangerous, so far beyond the bounds of propriety. I fear her reputation is spoiled, and she will be known as a young lady who will give up her virtue for a bit of pleasure."

"I can see how the idea pains you, but you must not worry about the threat to her reputation. Only a few members of our family know of the escapade, and they have too much affection for you all to spread vile rumors."

"I hope so, but people, especially servants, will talk, there is no escaping that fact."

Mr. Darcy's brow furrowed with a new thought. "Is it possible she has been corrupted by a servant—her maid, perhaps? An unreliable servant can sometimes convince a young lady to behave with more daring than she might act otherwise."

Sir Lewis shook his head. "Such a thing is not possible in this case. Dobbie has been in my family for decades and loves Anne like a daughter. In fact, I believe that Dobbie, more than anyone, is capable of setting Anne on the proper course, for she is a good-hearted soul with nary a vice in her. None of the servants are at fault." He drained the last of his port. "It's Fitzwilliam I worry about. Have you spoken to him?"

"Not yet. I wanted to speak first with you."

"It is a delicate situation. He must be pained to see how little affection and respect Anne holds for him that she would compromise herself with Mr. Wickham, of all men. Please know that I would not have Fitzwilliam's good nature assaulted for the world." Sir Lewis stood to take his leave. "A man I knew at Oxford hid a sly and manipulative character behind a handsome face and appealing manners. His dishonorable nature did not prevent him from being elected to Parliament. Such men often rise to positions of the highest calling in business, the clergy, and government. I am sorry to think Mr. Wickham might be such a man. I had expected better of him."

Mr. Darcy put out his hand, which Sir Lewis shook with a powerful grasp. "I hope his character can be improved, but today it seems I must deal with a wayward godson."

"I understand. Please inform Fitzwilliam that Anne will apologize to him. Are you available for a carriage ride tomorrow morning? … Good. The four of us will ride in one carriage and the young lovers can sort themselves in the other."

With those words he called for his coat and hat, leaving Mr. Darcy to consider how fraught was the challenge of raising a man of honor. He wondered, too, whether a man's nature was formed at birth or if it could be shaped by good examples and strong principles.

Chapter 20

A Traitor to Truth

Fitzwilliam found little natural beauty in Hyde Park. In winter its filthy Serpentine meandered through two fields of sparse wood and thin grass harvested by mangy sheep; its supposedly pastoral scene was marred by decaying lime trees and a roughly-hewn brick guard room, all blighting the eye.

Today any beauty it hoped to claim stood newly shorn, for tree barbers had pruned several dead trees of nearly all their branches, leaving a nest of woody material strewn across the grounds. Thin sunlight pushing its way through low, gray clouds did little to improve the park's appearance or lift his mood.

He rode with his cousin Anne in the Darcy carriage, the two of them seated side by side, a rug laid over his companion's lap to warm her legs. His parents and aunt and uncle followed in the carriage behind. There was no escaping their scrutiny.

He had spent the morning trying to decide how to handle himself. The path toward ease and comfort seemed narrowed by encroaching hedges and darkened by expectations. His father had warned him: "Sir Lewis expects Anne to apologize to you on our drive this morning. I know I can rely on you to be gracious, both in facilitating her show of regret—one might say, shame—and in accepting her overture, however poorly worded. You are more mature than she is and will know how to guide her if she proves shy."

One might say, recalcitrant, Fitzwilliam thought, feeling at a loss as to how to proceed.

"This is a most distressing situation, on all sides. No matter our thoughts about George's inexcusable behavior, we cannot allow this opportunity to pass. Your mother and I believe your engagement serves both of our families and want you and Anne to reach some sort of accord today. I know any worry on my side is misplaced, for you will do your duty."

A buffet to his son's shoulder sealed their pact.

Now Fitzwilliam stared ahead into the shorn and leafless trees bunched to one side of the drive. He felt quite tired—tired of George Wickham, tired of duty, tired of London. But the greatest of these was Wickham. The wretch gave no thought to the cost of his philandering. He did not care that his godfather felt bound to apologize to hurt friends and neighbors and sometimes to soothe the families of maids and villagers. Wickham, the snake, overlooked the embarrassment he caused the Darcy family and pursued his own happy way, seemingly determined to seduce every lady he met. He held cheap his family name and would not reform himself.

"I believe we must speak of Mr. Wickham," said a reluctant Fitzwilliam, who feared the carriage ride would end without the principals achieving the stated goal.

"Yes, so I've been told. I admit to not having understood his character and wonder: Is he always so free with his affection?"

Fitzwilliam looked down on his cousin.

Her face was small and pale, a child's face framed by a white straw bonnet *à-la-Pamela*. Any minute she might pick her nose like she used to do when she was eight or ten years old and her family joined the Darcys at their parish church. Was this not how he often thought of her, fidgeting in the family pew while she probed her nose to relieve the snuffles? A good elbowing made her behave. If only that would work now. If only he had known what was coming. A swift elbow to the side and she would keep her opinions about their engagement to herself. A poke to the ribs might remind her that no benefit accrued from favoring a rogue like Wickham over himself. A hard jab and she would repent with tears and regret for succumbing to Wickham's love-making.

If only they were still children … if only these imaginings had substance … if only a new, troubling image had not replaced the old one: Anne with bright, playful eyes and a single long braid covering one breast.

He had never glimpsed this creature; never beheld such a breathless and dreamy look on her face; never pictured her braided and beribboned hair snaking across her high bosom, falling nearly to her waist. He never imagined her submitting passionately to a man's love-making, but he had seen evidence of it, no matter the contrite look she gave her father. He was at once fascinated and disgusted with Wickham and with *her*. But how should he reply to her question? What could he say about Wickham's character that would not wound her further? His abiding sense of honor would not allow him to belittle or ridicule her, however so much he was tempted. Should he lie to her? Was a lie, however kindly meant, not also a fresh injury?

He caught her studying his face and felt discomfited by her open, steady gaze. "Have you read *The History of Sir Charles Grandison*?" he asked.

Anne observed that he did not answer her question about Wickham. "Yes, more than once. Did you read it?"

"I did, not that I wanted to do so. My former tutor, Mr.

Kerby, insisted that I read it, partly because it remains popular and partly because he believed my sphere of reading should encompass more than the Classics. Mr. Kerby believed I might learn something from the novel. In any event, you will recall the story. Miss Harriet Byron was an heiress, like yourself—"

"And a great beauty, which I am not."

Fitzwilliam squirmed at this proclamation, for Anne knew how to upset his equilibrium. Why did she make a comment to which there was no gracious reply? Did she expect him to deny it?

He did not look at her but carried on as if he had not heard her comment. "Among Miss Byron's several admirers were a few whose behavior was a little beyond the line of pleasing. Is that not so?"

"True. Mr. Greville was much enamored with her, believing her nose and mouth and forehead and complexion and eyes were all perfection, which is nonsense—no one is perfect, not even Miss Derrythorpe, whose ears are a little too large for her face, in my opinion. And then there was Sir Hargrave Pollexfen, who was very bold in his speeches to Miss Byron, after which he kidnapped her."

"Exactly so. Miss Byron was not impressed by any of the men who flattered her. Not until she came to know Sir Charles Grandison did she appreciate the virtues of a good man. His sense of honor and duty account for his being considered a fine figure of a moral man and an ideal lover." He caught Anne's bonnet bobbing up and down in agreement.

"And what did your reading teach you?" she asked, her eyes searching his profile. The lilt in her voice suggested a challenge.

"It taught me that kidnapping young ladies is no proper way to earn their affection."

Anne laughed, a quick warble of delight. "A good lesson learned."

He stared at her, astonished to hear her laugh at his meagre spark of humor, for he knew himself to be rather formal and not given to bursts of wit. Cousin Richard often chided him for being so serious, against which fault Fitzwilliam defended himself, but Richard had once told him that Anne loved a laugh and was easily amused.

So it seemed now, but then she seemed to tense.

"I suppose you expect me to offer my lesson learned from Richardson's novel," Anne said, "which is this: young ladies living fifty years ago were given to fainting and weeping fits when kidnapped. I might do the same, although I would hope for more gumption."

She left unsaid any mention of the difference between Miss Byron's situation and her own. Miss Byron's family and friends agreed she could marry a man of her own choosing, whereas she, the heiress of Rosings, could not.

She would marry Fitzwilliam, as was her duty. And, unlike Miss Byron, she would never have a dozen men fawning over her every utterance or falling on their knees, begging for her hand in marriage. She was not pretty enough to excite such admiration.

But these would be abominable things to say to Fitzwilliam, for how could he deny the truth of them?

As it was, she could neither defend nor explain herself to one so sensitive about Mr. Wickham. Fitzwilliam, she suspected, regularly found himself diminished by Mr. Wickham's good looks and easy, unaffected manners. It must peeve him no end to observe the son of his father's steward succeeding where he did not.

Regardless, she had been told to apologize for succumbing to charm and should do so now. "By anyone's standards, I behaved badly. I was deceived in Mr. Wickham's character and allowed myself to be flattered."

This is as close as she will come to offering an apology, thought Fitzwilliam. He could not fault her reticence, however, for it must be a bruise to her esteem to have succumbed to Wickham's seduction and under her father's nose.

Anne realized she was making a mess of it. A part of her wanted merely to be done with it, but equally she could not bear the idea that her cousin thought poorly of her. Perhaps for the first time she sought his good opinion, saying in a small voice, "I am sorry to have distressed you or caused you pain."

Her simple honesty was a surprise and therefore the more valuable.

Fitzwilliam was led to be more gracious toward her. "Wickham's behavior should not please any woman who respects herself," he told her, "but he often does please. He is drawn to the thrill of the chase, if you understand my meaning, like hounds after a fox. Flattery is a kind of sport with him, and he uses it to his advantage."

"Yes, I believe Mr. Wickham's pretty words scattered my wits."

She felt a traitor to truth to confess regret over the scandal, for she had allowed Mr. Wickham to impose himself on her. The prospect of a romantic adventure had thrilled her, bringing her alive in a way she had never felt. Receiving his gentle smiles and caressing looks had been no hardship, for she felt flattered and special under his congenial eye. His seduction had been willingly sought and longed for.

If Fitzwilliam were to be believed, she did not respect herself because she found Mr. Wickham's behavior pleasing. This thinking presented a puzzle, for even though she had been caught in a compromising situation, she did not disrespect herself. She had acted—too boldly, too intemperately, fair enough—on strong feelings of attraction that felt right and good. Whether Fitzwilliam or his parents or her parents accepted the fact or not, it was true that she felt desired by Mr. Wickham, which led her to wonder whether she might ever feel desired by Fitzwilliam.

"Wickham will make a mess of some young lady's life one day, of that I am sure," Fitzwilliam was saying.

"I hope you are wrong about him. Will he attend Sir Robert's ball next week? I ask so that I can be prepared to meet with him again."

"It has not yet been decided."

Chapter 21

The Warm Hopes of Youth

The next days were a misery. When visiting family, Anne forced a smile, joined in conversations, and behaved as expected. These she did with a heavy heart. Whether sipping tea with aunt Fitzwilliam or playing cards with her cousins, she seemed to sit apart, like a low actor in a stage play. She felt marked, as if some sign, formerly invisible, now shone to all and sundry: willful child, schemer, harlot.

Yet she also felt her family's approbation. No one turned a shoulder, no one whispered discreetly to a companion, no one gave her a malevolent stare, no one was uncivil. Her uncle and aunt Darcy remained stalwart in their tender feelings. Receiving their generous affection bruised her heart all the more, for they must question their decision to marry their son to his cousin.

Strangely, Lady Catherine's tongue had been stilled. Her ladyship refrained from criticizing and correcting her behavior, which made Anne wonder whether, in fact, her tryst with Mr. Wickham had finally pushed her beyond the circle of amendment, such that her character was now fixed as selfish and disobedient. Only the worst sort of person would shock and wound a mother so deeply. Only a truly bad person would offend her intended, a man widely admired for his worthy principles and high ideals.

Despite her sincere apology, Fitzwilliam barely noticed her when they were in company together, but in this his behavior differed little from any other time. And Mr. Wickham had not joined their plans for several days now, which suggested a punishment for his bad behavior. Perhaps he had been sent down to Pemberley. She had not the courage to ask, and she avoided the library, that too-near den of iniquity, until summoned there one morning by Sir Lewis.

"Sit here, Anne. I must ask you a question."

Anne felt awkward stepping into her father's realm. His manner toward her had been cool of late, leading her to fear some part of his affection had been lost forever. On his command, none the less, she took her favorite chair, sitting demurely with her back to the windows overlooking the garden and mews.

"Your mother and I received a letter from Mrs. Ormiston, who invites us to join her family, along with the Fitzwilliams, the Darcys, and the Dighursts, for a dinner and musical program. I mention this to you because it is likely that Mr. Wickham will attend. Lady Catherine and I have discussed the situation and conclude that you shall join us. We do not fear any repeat of the awful circumstances in which you found yourself with Mr. Wickham when he was a guest here, but we wish to warn you of his expected attendance. Do you believe yourself ready to meet him in public?"

"Yes, Papa."

"Good. We would not impose on you if we did not believe you mature enough to manage yourself in company. Miss Waygood will accompany us, and I believe Miss and Mr.

Derrythorpe will also attend. You will have many friends there to entertain you."

"Yes, Papa."

She did not tarry but returned upstairs, where she could sit and consider this intelligence. She picked up a tattered copy of the *Rambler*. Opening the periodical at random she read: "Such is the condition of life, that something is always wanting to happiness. In youth we have warm hopes, which are soon blasted by rashness and negligence, and great designs which are defeated by inexperience."

These words might have been written for her. They should calm her nerves and remove any suffering at the prospect of meeting her lover, for that is how Mr. Wickham stood in her heart and mind. If only she could abide by Dr. Johnson's reminder about warm hopes, she might achieve something akin to contentment. It was not possible. She could think of nothing but the misery of meeting a man she loved but from whom she would be always separated.

In the end her staunchest allies, cousin Richard and Mr. Derrythorpe, petted and teased her throughout the Ormiston's dinner and got her through the worst of it.

Mr. Wickham was seated far along the table from where Anne sat. Once or twice she glanced in his direction, but he paid her no heed. This itself was a wound. His careless indifference suggested his love-making meant nothing to him, that she was nothing to him.

She pushed a bit of crimped cod around her plate with a fork and listened to cousin Richard's discourse on Napoleon's supposed strategies after Britain declared war on France. Eventually, Mr. Derrythorpe captured her attention with his opinions about the Leverian Museum's fossils and corals. She relished his boyish enthusiasm, knowing she would miss his company when her family returned to Kent.

After dinner the party moved into a large saloon for dancing and music. A pianist had been hired for the evening, which relieved Miss Derrythorpe and Miss Waygood from having to perform.

Miss Derrythorpe approached Anne, saying, "Would you enjoy a lesson in how to win a lover?"

Anne flushed, fearing the Beauty had learned of her illicit rendezvous with Mr. Wickham, but perceiving Miss Derrythorpe's manner as natural and unguarded, she said, "Of course. You must show me how it is to be done. Which gentleman will you choose?"

"Why, my cousin Charles, of course."

"You jest. Charles Fitzwilliam cares only about his horses and hounds and politics. He will never be your lover."

"True, but I can make him offer for my hand in the next dance. Do you doubt it?"

"Charles dislikes dancing, as you will soon discover."

Miss Derrythorpe smiled sweetly and moved next to Charles, who stood talking to Major Dighurst. With complete confidence, Miss Derrythorpe insinuated herself into their conversation and inserted a comment that made the men laugh. She succeeded in playing the coquette. Charles led her into the set, where he joined his brother, Richard, who partnered Miss Ormiston, and also Mrs. Dighurst, who was paired with Sir Lewis.

Anne was acknowledging Miss Derrythorpe's conquering smile when Fitzwilliam approached.

"Anne, may I have the honor of your hand for this dance?"

She felt peeved by his gallantry. Although she wished it, she could not fault him for being a gentleman. Their families wanted to see them dancing and talking and acting like an engaged couple should act. Believing the whole room watched them, she smiled and accepted his hand.

"I am pleased to see you smile. We are not enemies, are we?"

"Of course not," she replied, thinking: we aren't friends either. She wondered what he thought of her. His face betrayed no disgust, but it revealed no affection either.

When the set ended she chose a chair and watched a new set form. Miss Waygood, radiating energy and good humor, partnered Mr. Wickham. He cut a fine figure and flirted easily. Anne watched him talking and laughing, his manners so charming as to make even Miss Waygood relent, such that all her criticism of Mr. Wickham seemed forgotten. Anne felt a strike of pain to see with what practiced manners Mr. Wickham conquered Miss Waygood's resistance. He charmed. She succumbed. Might he succeed in seducing her?

Just as this question formed, Mrs. Ormiston took the seat next to her.

"I enjoyed your dancing," she said as the couples changed partners. "You and Mr. Darcy make a charming couple. Do you find his manners agreeable?"

"He is a handsome man with perfect manners," Anne admitted, much to her chagrin, for these were precisely the characteristics her mother found so endearing in him. "He can be agreeable in my company, but he appears most at ease among his intimates. I cannot claim to understand him well, even though we are cousins."

"That is not surprising," remarked Mrs. Ormiston, "for he is still a young man beginning to make his way in society. It is a trying time for him, just as it is for you." She patted Anne's arm with her fan.

The two of them observed the dancers, who seemed to have a game afoot. Fitzwilliam changed partners to dance with Miss Derrythorpe, while Mr. Wickham took Miss Ormiston as a partner. Mr. Wickham seemed to have found the perfect partner, for his silly comments drew a steady stream of giggles from her. At one point their laughter rang loudly over the notes of the pianoforte. Mrs. Ormiston seemed unperturbed by her daughter's clownish behavior.

"What of Mr. Wickham? Do you find him pleasing?"

"I admire his merry eye, although I do not understand his character." Anne could only hope her neighbor detected no hidden sensibilities. She was fond of Mrs. Ormiston and would not wish her to know about her tryst with Mr. Wickham.

"Fortunately, you have many years in which to acquire an understanding of men. Let the effort be your challenge, and if you comprehend one, please share your view with the rest of us, for men can be most provoking. No creature's behavior is more mysterious and inscrutable than man's. Excuse me, I shall speak with Clarinda." Mrs. Ormiston rose to tame her daughter's exuberance.

Anne considered her neighbor's comments. Was there no middle ground between these two men?

She glanced from Mr. Wickham to Fitzwilliam. For all his handsome features and regal bearing, Fitzwilliam was mostly humorless and often haughty. She wondered how her cousin could be always so serious, so lofty in his ideals, so bound by duty. His sensibilities did not seem natural for a young man of nineteen years. More importantly, he seemed to have little regard for her. Privately, she had admitted to Tilly that she did not warm to him.

"Do you think he is aware of the marriage pact you suspect was made between your mothers?" Tilly had asked before the de Bourghs departed Rosings for London. She and Anne had been ensconced in the music room at Rosings, where they sat embroidering pillow-covers.

"I cannot be certain. He has never spoken of it."

"If he is aware of it, his aloofness and reserve might be proof of uncertainty regarding his betrothal to you."

"You think he resents it?" Anne asked, it being a question she pondered regularly.

"Possibly. More likely, he simply does not like you." Tilly grinned and made no effort to avoid the plump pillow tossed in her direction.

Anne wondered if Tilly's joking insight held a grain of truth. Fitzwilliam might feel no felicity with her, just as she found no desire in herself for him. She could see, though, that he was enjoying himself with the radiant Miss Derrythorpe, even venturing to converse with her during the dance. His face glowed with admiration and approval.

For herself, prepared as she was to admit to little experience in matters of the heart, Mr. Wickham was the more interesting and provocative man. The memory of his kisses made her pulse race.

The memory of her father's rebuke brought a heart ache.

Chapter 22

A Hopeless Case

"That scowl would kill a horse."

Richard studied his companion's profile, thinking Fate had been cruel to bestow all the manly graces on his cousin's face while leaving his own plain as an old shoe. Where his cousin's smile charmed, his own smile was deformed by crooked teeth; where Darcy was tall with strong shoulders, he himself was neither tall nor short, lean nor fat. Nothing about his visage was exceptional. He was a common side dish to Darcy's elegant dessert.

"Hmm?" Darcy murmured.

I said, "That owl would swill a gorse."

At these words Darcy turned, his frown deepening. "That makes no sense."

"I know it, but I hoped to say something that would pull you back from the brink. These past ten minutes you have been treading some netherworld. I feared you might disappear—a phantasm."

"That is not possible—at least, not while I sit here before the fire, all safe and sound."

"True. It is neither possible nor likely but a worry none the less. Do you care to share your thoughts?" Richard could perfectly well guess what was troubling his cousin, but he chose not to raise the subject for fear of discomfiting him. Darcy—he had never called him Fitzwilliam—was not one to share his innermost thoughts.

It had always been thus, starting when they were boys, each coming to understand the other: Darcy, the heir; Richard, a second son. No matter that he, not Darcy, was the son of an earl, it was Darcy whose person bore the stamp of future landowner. Had their distinct positions affected their relations? They were companionable cousins but not close. They had grown into manhood with expectations of duty but had never discussed them. Their relationship was cordial but not confiding. Even so, there was goodwill between them, and that was all that mattered.

Darcy sipped a full-bodied port, pleased to receive comfort from so simple a pleasure, and considered whether he wished to address the topic that held him captive. It was a delicate issue and possibly not one to be brought into the sunlight like a potted flower.

The cousins had retired to the library in Lord Matlock's house after an evening spent first at the Opera House and later at Boodle's Club, where Richard had joined a table of faro. Luck was running in his favor, for he made several winning bets and lost track of time. Darcy had sat in an over-large chair near a window in deep conversation with his friend Brid. There he remained until Richard suggested they return to St. James's Square for a glass of some blood-warming brew to guard against the threat of snow.

"What did Brid have to say for himself?" Richard asked, thinking a change of subject might help. "Does he have some new scheme afoot?"

Here was a topic Darcy could warm to. "His father is planning another expedition to Egypt, perhaps the year after next. Brid has invited me to join them."

"I say, Darcy! That would be an incredible adventure. You always hoped to take a tour, but did you imagine traveling to Egypt—and so soon after Napoleon's departure?"

"Brid told me his father believes that while there is no love there for the French, the country is not particularly hostile to the British. The biggest worry is the infighting among the Turks, Albanians, and the Egyptian Mamluks. An outright civil war might delay the expedition, and, of course, I do not know whether my father will consider the offer. He expects me to finish my studies at Cambridge, but he might view the trip favorably, especially as I would travel with Lord Bridlestowe and several British scientists. I won't stoke my hopes just yet, as a lot can happen in two years."

With these words he fell under his former morose spell and stared into the fire. Richard was prepared to wait.

Eventually Darcy said, "What, in your opinion, is required to be happy?"

Richard laughed. "Money! I thought you understood that." If this is where the conversation began, it promised to be a long night.

Darcy shook his head as if clearing cobwebs. "Wealth eases one's way in life, but it isn't sufficient by itself. I am interested in knowing what you require in the way of a wife."

A crude joke came to mind, but on seeing Darcy's earnest expression, Richard governed his tongue. "Of course, you, being an heir, would think money merely sufficient, whereas I, a second son, must think of money as a lifeblood matter." His grin was meant to take the sting out of his words, for he and his cousin stood in very different realms. "I believe, like you, that I am expected to marry an heiress. I hope to find one with a pleasing countenance—I do not aim for beauty, for what handsome woman would marry a common-looking fellow such as myself?—and she must have agreeable manners, a sparkling wit, a small waist"—here he held his hands up to fashion a smallish circle—"and a soft, generous bosom!"

The cousins laughed together, easing the tension in the room.

"And yourself?" Richard asked. "You must be thinking of Anne." He feared he might have spoken too boldly and held his breath while waiting for a response.

Darcy nodded. "I am thinking of her and wondering what to do about our engagement."

"You do not wish it."

His cousin's words, spoken so softly, so matter-of-factly, stung Darcy to his core. "I do not wish it, and I don't think she does either. We find ourselves in a quandary, for neither of us is prepared to distress our parents or fail in our duty. I can see no way forward that does not bring heartache and trouble to one or both of us." With a heavy sigh he added, "Last winter I had a dream about Anne … a dream in which she died before we could marry." He lifted his eyes to catch his cousin's reaction. "On awakening I was briefly disoriented but then felt ashamed, for I had felt joy, true joy. I had been released, by what power I cannot say, from a duty I found repugnant. I only know that I felt relief. What kind of man does that make me? My heart is so black that I would wish my intended dead. I would rob her of life itself for my own comfort and pleasure. I am a sorry specimen."

"You are human, Darcy, and it was a mere dream," Richard shot back, ever ready to lessen his cousin's torment and defend his honor. "Your situation is unusual in that you have been engaged to Anne since infancy, the decision not even yours to make. It cannot be easy to manage the expectation of an arranged marriage, whether you've known of it for years or only a few weeks, although many youths do submit to their parents' wishes where marriage is concerned. Only think of my parents and Lady Catherine and Sir Lewis. None of them had a choice. But times are changing. Today many of us expect or, at least, hope to choose a spouse based on the prospect of affection or love. You should talk to Charles. His mission is to find a worthy wife before our parents arrange a wedding for him. He attends every ball, every dance and assembly, every supper and card party to which he is invited, all with the aim of meeting a woman who will please him and be acceptable to our parents. That is the condition."

"The condition?" asked a confused Darcy.

"Yes. When our mother began promoting the third daughter of Lord Tuesley as a potential wife and hinted that some discussions had already taken place, Charles became distressed. He negotiated—there is no better word for it—the opportunity to find a wife of rank and quality by his own effort. He has been granted two years in which to do so. If at the end of two years he is still unmarried, then my parents will seek a spouse for him, and they are allowed to introduce him to any young lady they believe is acceptable."

"I had no idea Lord Matlock was so progressive and hardly credit their agreement, for I know how much Charles hates parties and balls. Would that I had the wherewithal for so bold an approach. Can you imagine my trying to negotiate with Lady Catherine? She's about as movable as a mountain."

Richard readily agreed. "Negotiating with the likes of our aunt would require the most consummate diplomacy. I wouldn't wager even Thomas Bruce could succeed with her, despite—"

Darcy smiled at last. "You don't think the Earl of Elgin could win her over?"

"No. Lord Elgin can soothe the Ottomans, but he'll never move your mother or your aunt. Their positions are fixed, like the sun and moon. At least with Anne, you know enough of her character and situation to have no worries." On seeing Darcy's startled look, he said, "Is there a problem?"

"I don't know Anne at all. I don't seem to have much to say to her, and she is usually skittish and reserved and sometimes grouchy when we are together."

"Anne? Skittish and reserved? Grouchy? You must be joking. I would never describe her in those terms."

"That doesn't surprise me. She's different with you."

Richard knew not what to say to help him see another side of her. "There is some truth in your assessment, for I noticed it myself, but I hope you will learn to appreciate her depth. She isn't an empty-headed woman with more hair than wit. Her head isn't filled with nonsense and overly romantic inclinations. She's clever, as clever as you in many respects, and were she not a woman, she might best many a man at university. You know Sir Lewis. He's been introducing her to the Classics and articles in *The Gentleman's Magazine* for years. I daresay she's read every issue from front to back and can speak on any topic mentioned there." Richard paused, trying to read the expression on Darcy's face. "What did I say to give you such a look?"

Darcy shook his head.

"Come, man. Speak. We are discussing your future and your hope for happiness."

Giving his cousin a level stare, Darcy asked, "Have you been told of Anne's indiscretion with Wickham?"

"Anne and Wickham? I don't believe it!"

"It is true. Sir Lewis and I discovered them in the Chidham House library together, alone. It was an awkward moment, to say the least. Fortunately, their passion had not progressed beyond a few kisses."

He recalled the image of her standing next to Wickham: breathless, her long braid hanging loose, her eyes aglow. He could not express his fear that, were it not for being discovered, their passion might very well have taken flight. This was a painful memory, best kept to himself. "She is justly contrite and keeps her distance from me and from him, but her behavior has shocked everybody."

"Surely she cannot be blamed for Wickham's seduction. He had the upper hand, I am sure of it."

"You are right there, but she was a willing participant in his scheme. There was no mistaking her look. She sought the tryst as much as he."

Richard rubbed the polish on one of his boots. "She is very young. Some allowance can be made for her ignorance of such matters. By the time you return from your grand tour of Egypt, you may feel differently. She may as well."

"I don't know," Darcy said solemnly. "It seems a hopeless case."

"No, not hopeless. Never hopeless. A lot can happen in two years. Anne has more gumption than you give her credit for. If she decides she doesn't want to marry *you*, believe me, she'll find a way out of her dilemma. Lord Elgin is no match for Lady Catherine, but I suspect Anne might be."

"Care to place a bet on that?" Darcy asked.

Richard grinned. "Make an offer. I'm feeling lucky."

Chapter 23

This Great Oaf

The looking-glass returned Anne's stare, reflecting a young lady wearing a fashionable silk dress the color of honey. Its puffed sleeves and beaded bodice trimmed with white lace complemented her slender frame.

"You look a proper lady. Very pretty, indeed," said Dobbie.

Anne gave her maid a sly look. Dobbie had never spoken of her encounter with Mr. Wickham in the library. Dobbie's spirit was kind and forgiving and nothing like that of the hall footmen, who had probably shared all sorts of false stories with the Chidham House staff.

The thought of being the topic of such lurid speculation made Anne wince. In the aftermath of that ignoble evening, as time and common sense worked on her heart, the memory of Mr. Wickham's kisses and passionate embrace brought little joy and was superseded by the image of her father's frowning countenance and sharp reprimand.

"You are kind to say so," she told Dobbie. "I hope to dance often, for I believe Sir Robert has hired an orchestra to entertain his guests."

Miss Derrythorpe had spoken of little else but Sir Robert's ball in the past week—what gown she planned to wear, how she would fix her hair, who would attend, who she might be introduced to. "It shall be the most exciting event. Only think of all the young men who shall offer to stand up with us."

Anne struggled to support her friend's enthusiasm, and now that the evening had arrived, her stomach seized at the thought of being in company again with Mr. Wickham. Very likely he would ignore her, as he had done at the Ormistons' musical evening, which thought confused her, for although she was mostly appalled by her behavior, she did sometimes miss the thrill of the chase, as Fitzwilliam had put it.

Perhaps she had been more in love with the idea of Mr. Wickham than with the man himself. Sir Robert's ball might decide her heart's true understanding.

The evening began well.

Anne enjoyed observing the antics of Miss Derrythorpe's many admirers. Mr. Galway made a nuisance of himself, being struck dumb by her beauty and hardly willing to leave her side except when another gentleman invited her to join a set.

A few of the Beauty's castoffs were so bold as to ask Miss de Bourgh to dance, which offers she accepted as a means of lassoing her thoughts about Mr. Wickham.

Some few hours later Anne chatted with Mr. Gregson, the eldest son of the vicar of Knebworth parish in Hertfordshire. He was short and portly and wore the eager smile of a man comfortable in his own skin. While he regaled her with stories of the antics of his eight siblings, her eye surveyed the crowd.

With nearly two hundred guests in attendance, the room had grown stifling. The air smelled of perfume mingled with sweat.

She had been introduced to several interesting men, including, of course, Sir Robert's son, Mr. William Alfriston-Seal, known as Alfrit. He led her into a dance, perhaps acting on duty, where his queer manners were disturbing, for he spoke not a word during the set. In form he was of average height and muscular, but his features failed to please. His pale eyes shone with barely contained contempt; his cruel mouth sported a crooked smile; his square jaw and florid cheeks were not flattered by a haircut in the Brutus style. His appearance was altogether menacing. As they paired during the dance his beefy, sweaty hand squeezed her own, almost to the point of pain.

She had never enjoyed a partner less.

"Do you know our host well?" asked Mr. Gregson as he observed the dancers.

"Please forgive me. My thoughts wandered." Watching Mr. Wickham smile down on a young lady to whom Anne had not been introduced was surprisingly painful.

"I wondered whether you know Sir Robert well."

"No, I cannot say that I do. He is a neighbor of my uncle Mr. Darcy. I was introduced to Sir Robert this evening."

"My family is a little acquainted with his. We are better acquainted with the Darcys."

"I was not aware that you knew them. Do you know the son?"

"We entered Cambridge together. I cannot claim to know Mr. Darcy well, for our families have met only a few times and mostly on Sunday, but I admire what I see. He sets a good example by being polite and studious. He's a rare, good fellow in my view, being quite intelligent and generous with his time. I rely on him to help with my Greek translations, without which instruction I would be lost."

Praise, indeed, thought Anne.

"Miss de Bourgh, would you honor me with the next dance?"

The moment was upon her before she was ready for it. Mr. Wickham waited for her reply.

"Yes, thank you."

She gave Mr. Gregson an apologetic smile and took Mr. Wickham's hand. She could not read the expression on his face but resolved to enjoy herself. Her effort was for naught, for he said little of consequence to her during the dance. His demeanor bordered on the haughty; his countenance, impossible to read; his smile, insincere.

When the dance ended, he pulled her a little to one side, near an open window. "You do not appear quite well. Indeed, I believe you have lost your bloom, which happens often enough when one is in Town."

"I am well, thank you."

Wickham looked puzzled. "Indeed, if you say so, but it disturbs me to see both you and Fitz in such despairing moods. Fitz, of course, is challenged by a special worry, of which you are the cause."

Anne recoiled at his words. "Whatever do you mean?"

"You may have noticed his attraction to Miss Derrythorpe. He quickly fell under her charm at your uncle's card party. You observed how his eyes followed her about the room, and how excited he was when she chose him for her table. Yet, he seemed not to please her, for I later thought her disappointed in his performance, so much so that her attention was attracted elsewhere. You understand, he is not accustomed to having a pretty lady scorn his fine visage and show no interest in his person."

Wickham sighed. "And now his engagement to you is widely known among the family and perhaps beyond, and he must face his duty. It is a worry for him. You understand this, I'm sure."

Anne was stunned, for she had detected Fitzwilliam's attraction to the Beauty on several occasions in the past few weeks. She also feared he was not happy about his engagement.

"It's Fitz I worry about," Wickham continued. "He has been quite bad tempered of late, owing perhaps to his viewing your engagement with little pleasure. He hinted as much to me recently."

"You are teasing me, for I know enough of your relationship with Fitzwilliam to know he would never share a confidence with you."

An indignant scowl flashed across Wickham's face before disappearing behind a mask of charm. "Not as a rule, it is true, but when we are thrown together, as we have been in Town, we sometimes speak of our lives and worries."

"Worries? What worries could either of you have? He has begun his studies at Cambridge and enjoys a life to which he is well suited, and you are here in Town, which is a balm to soothe your frustration with country living. You shouldn't presume to know how either Fitzwilliam or I feel. Pray excuse me."

She escaped further scrutiny and went into the tearoom, where she forced herself to drink a rather tepid cup of tea. What an impudent trickster! He enjoyed tormenting her and possessed an expert's eye in reading people's weaknesses, for he had identified her and Fitzwilliam's unease regarding their engagement. How like him to act on his impressions with nefarious intent.

After the next set was underway, she rejoined the dancers in the main saloon. She was imagining Mr. Wickham telling tales to his friends about their sordid romp in the Chidham House library when Mr. Derrythorpe touched her arm.

"Have you seen my sister?"

"Not recently. She was dancing the cotillion with Mr. Gregson when I went for tea."

"I fear she is up to her old tricks, for I cannot find her in the tearoom, nor is she sitting with aunt Fitzwilliam, Lady Anne, or Lady Catherine." While he spoke his eyes flitted from couple to couple in search of his sister. "Would you help me survey the dancers? Perhaps I lost her in the crowd."

"Of course. I'll go this way and meet you back here."

Anne circled around the main saloon, endeavoring to look as though she found the dancers enchanting while also taking care to smile at various acquaintances.

She spoke briefly with Miss Ormiston and her brother Lawrence, after which she passed a distressed Mr. Derrythorpe, whose face was full of worry. A crush of people encircled the dance floor, making progress difficult, but she was not deterred. "I failed to find her," she told Mr. Derrythorpe on her return.

His grimace relayed defeat as well. "May I impose on your good nature to help me search for her upstairs?"

"Would it not serve you better to ask Richard or Charles to accompany you?"

"I would prefer for them not to know of my concern. They believe Maria to be a most exemplary young lady. I would not have them learn otherwise if I can avoid it."

Anne paled at his words, for she realized he would not consider herself a modest young lady if he knew of her secret meeting with Mr. Wickham. It pained her to make this discovery, but this was not the time to think about her reputation. She should strive to relieve his distress.

"Surely your concern is for naught."

"We can only hope," he said grimly before leading her through the throng toward the front of the house, where they passed revelers clustered in the hall. Even here the noise was deafening.

She followed him up the wide, elegant stairs to the private apartments, feeling guilty at trespassing in Sir Robert's house and wondering whether any of the guests observed them mounting the stairs together. The footman at the top of the stairs stood rigid as a statue and did not ask their business.

"Wait here." Mr. Derrythorpe walked the wide, carpeted hall, pausing briefly to listen at every door.

"Let's go up another floor. I must be confident that I have searched everywhere before speaking with my uncle."

Anne agreed and turned ahead of him up the staircase. Near the top she whispered, "Look, there is Mr. Alfriston-Seal."

The youth lounged against a tall door and chewed on a fingernail.

Mr. Derrythorpe pushed past Anne and strode down the hall. Mr. Alfriston-Seal, aware of movement, said, "Ah, what do you two do here? This is a private floor, you must know."

"Where is my sister?"

"I am sure I do not know. Perhaps she submitted to Mr. Galway's love-making." He snorted, as if at a neat joke.

Mr. Derrythorpe shoved the man aside and tried opening the door. Mr. Alfriston-Seal shoved back. "Oy! You cannot come up here, pushing your way around."

Fearing a rumpus, Anne retreated to the ballroom. Her eyes scanned the dancers and observants until she caught Fitzwilliam listening to the pretty but rapacious Miss Montgomery. Hesitating on the crowd's periphery, she studied him with a clarity that made her heart ache.

He stood a head above his fellow men, his shoulders squared. A fixed half-smile and wary look told her that he was not enjoying the lady's company. He looked so very elegant. A wave of pride surged through her. Here was her future husband and intimate partner. For a bold instant all things seemed possible. They could be happy together building a life and raising children. The moment lasted until he lifted his head and saw her, a look of inquiry (or was it irritation?) crossing his face. She approached, knowing time could not be lost.

"Excuse me," said Anne. "May I speak with you, cousin?" She smiled and used a pleasant, well-modulated voice so as not to invite Miss Montgomery's curiosity. Even a hint of a scandal could have far-reaching consequences.

Fitzwilliam read the plea in Anne's eyes. "Of course. Excuse us, Miss Montgomery." He took her elbow with a practiced motion and steered her toward the tearoom.

"Mr. Derrythorpe needs your help. May I take you to him? The situation is urgent."

Fitzwilliam raised an eyebrow but gave his consent.

As they ascended the stairs, she whispered, "Mr. Derrythorpe and I have been searching for his sister. He believes Mr. Alfriston-Seal guards a room where she may be sequestered. When I left to find you, an argument had broken out. Perhaps the issue has been resolved, but if it has not, I believe your presence will facilitate matters."

When they stepped onto the third story, they saw an adroit Mr. Derrythorpe dodge a swing from his host.

Fitzwilliam moved with the speed of a natural athlete. "Stop," he ordered as he grabbed Mr. Alfriston-Seal's arm. "It would be better to act the gentleman than the boor."

"This rogue," said a breathless Mr. Derrythorpe, "will not let me check this room."

Fitzwilliam wore his most formidable frown, which made Mr. Alfriston-Seal flinch a little. "Move."

"There is nothing to see," the besotted youth said, his words running together.

"If there is nothing to see, then you can have no grounds for preventing our entry."

Fitzwilliam thrust open the door and lead his companions into the gloom. The spectacle stopped the rescuers cold. On the high bed Miss Derrythorpe sat astride Mr. Wickham, her long hair hanging in loose curls, her gown rucked up about her knees. Mr. Wickham's hands encircled her waist. He looked both comfortable and content leaning against the puffy pillows.

"Oh, James!" she cried as she became aware of the intruders and rolled off to one side. "I feared you might not save me from this great oaf. He has been pestering me this past half-hour."

Mr. Alfriston-Seal laughed.

Mr. Derrythorpe gave him a sharp look before staring at his sister. "Pestering? You are the most shameless—"

Fitzwilliam intervened. "Let cooler heads prevail. Mr. Alfriston-Seal, you and Mr. Wickham are no longer wanted here."

A lazy Wickham slid off the bed and put his coat on. "I have been entertaining your favorite one, Fitz. I did not think you would mind. Come, Alfrit. We shall find more game below."

Fitzwilliam watched them go before saying to Mr. Derrythorpe: "Please believe me—I shall deal with Mr. Wickham later. Anne—"

"Truly, there is no need—" began Miss Derrythorpe. Her words trailed into nothingness on beholding Fitzwilliam's scowl.

"Anne, would you be willing to help Miss Derrythorpe restore herself before coming downstairs?"

"Of course."

"I suggest you do not dawdle. Let's return to the ballroom, Mr. Derrythorpe."

Anne understood. The couple's absence might already have been missed by any number of interested parties who would gladly share news of the indiscretion with their acquaintances.

When Fitzwilliam pulled closed the door, Miss Derrythorpe said, "Of all the hoity-toity—"

"You would do better to be grateful that Mr. Darcy and your brother rescued you," said Anne.

"Don't speak to me in that tone. I have done nothing wrong. In fact, there is no need for you to act so holy. Mr. Wickham and I are engaged."

"Yes, I can readily believe it. You are engaged in a dangerous bout of self-deception. Mr. Wickham is neither a decent nor honorable man, and your family will never agree to an engagement to a man with no steady income or prospects, especially after tonight's escapade."

Seeing the fury on the Beauty's face spurred Anne to be more gracious. "We cannot set this aright by arguing over spilled milk. Here, let me try to rearrange your hair. We must make you presentable."

Miss Derrythorpe wore a proud pout but submitted to Anne's ungainly efforts to restore her looks to something resembling a proper young lady.

When they entered the ballroom, Mr. Hamilton approached Miss Derrythorpe to join the dance. She accepted his invitation and smiled at Anne with nary an ounce of shame in her soul.

Chapter 24

Pain and a Posset

"You look fair tuckered out," said Dobbie as she bustled about, removing Anne's gown and chemise and laying out her nightclothes. "I had a fire laid, knowin' you'd be tired after dancing. Was the orchestra nice?"

"The music was lovely," Anne replied, almost by rote. "There was such a crush of guests, and more food than I've ever seen in one tearoom."

Dobbie, being an able reader of her charge's moods, refrained from pressing for more information. "I prepared a posset to help you sleep and asked Betsy to bring it up.—Ah, here she is. It is well after two o'clock and your head is spinnin' with music and conversations and visions of handsome young men. A ball can make one too tired to rest well." She set the posset on the bedside table. "I shall come wake you at noon if you are not stirrin' about. Sleep well, love."

Anne settled against the bed pillows, her hands wrapped around a cup of warmed milk spiced with cinnamon and wine. She sipped the posset and stared into the shadows, her spirit bruised by a single evening of anticipated merriment and ugly discovery. One and only one image filled her head: Mr. Wickham propped against the bed pillows, his dark eyes aglow, his face softened with admiration as he gazed with a lover's eyes on Miss Derrythorpe.

The intimate scene made Anne's heart hurt, for she had beheld delight and desire in Mr. Wickham's face. She had thought his melting look was meant only for her. What folly. What shame.

Everybody—Papa, Miss Waygood, Fitzwilliam—everybody but her own foolish self had discerned Mr. Wickham's true character. She alone had believed in his regard for her.

What must Fitzwilliam think? The poor man—to discover first his intended alone with Mr. Wickham, wallowing in illicit kisses, and then to find Miss Derrythorpe in an equally compromising situation. These images must bring him pain.

Had she been wrong to seek his help? Of course, she had not known beforehand that Miss Derrythorpe was secluded with Mr. Wickham or else she might have approached Richard. Even so, Fitzwilliam was the first person who came to mind when the argument erupted between Mr. Derrythorpe and their host's son. She knew her Clun friend could rely on Fitzwilliam's discretion, and there was no doubting her cousin's ability to handle Mr. Alfriston-Seal.

If she laid her heart open to honesty then she must admit that Fitzwilliam, for all his reserve and sometimes overbearing nature, was a decent and honorable man. Being a true gentleman, he had joined her cause with nary a qualm or question and taken control of the situation with one aim: protect Miss Derrythorpe's reputation. He had shown himself to be resolute and considerate.

These were attractive, even admirable qualities, but was mere admiration a sufficient basis for marriage? This was the unanswerable question.

Such rumination did not promote sleep. She placed her teacup on the bed-side table and threw off the bed cover. A little drawing might calm her thoughts. Moving the candle to her writing desk, she found a plain sheet of artist's paper and several pencils. What should be the object of her study? Her eye fell on Mr. Derrythorpe's ugly root. It would do. Pulling her wrapper over her shoulders she set to work, first drawing the lumpish outline of the bewhiskered root before sketching its shadow.

Her mind quietened before circling back to the awful scene of Miss Derrythorpe straddling Mr. Wickham's hips. The Beauty had bewitched the man with her wild hair cascading like inky ribbons down her back. Conjuring from thin air a ridiculous explanation for being found alone with him in an upstairs bedchamber, she probably hoped her rescuers would overlook her youth and forgive her impertinence.

It remained to be seen what punishment would be meted, but Mr. Wickham surely deserved some hideous penalty for the crime of being an incurable flirt. He was an indolent Man of Pleasure, a wily weasel who gave no thought to anyone's gratification but his own.

Unbidden, Miss Derrythorpe's words sprung to mind: "At the very least you will want to learn whether he knows how to kiss properly."

Oh, what an agony to recall these words, for Mr. Wickham proved to be a good kisser—a fact Miss Derrythorpe would readily support, no doubt. Never mind that Anne had no other experience of a lover's kiss. She accepted her instinct on the matter: Mr. Wickham was a skillful lover. Of course, possessing this skill, however much admired, did not lessen his many faults.

How had their assignation been arranged? Had Mr. Wickham merely raised an eyebrow to make known his wish? Or had he approached Miss Derrythorpe directly and laid bare his plan? Perhaps no natural acuity for deciphering his signal was needed—perhaps she had approached him! More likely they had relied on Mr. Alfriston-Seal's help, which, if true, in no way flattered his character. Regardless, nothing in their behavior had aroused suspicion. There had been no hints of corresponding tender looks, no certain change in their manners, no awkward encounters to incite censure. They paid each other no particular attention when in company, and yet had the determination to arrange a private meeting.

The most curious aspect of the debacle was that neither Miss Derrythorpe nor Mr. Wickham seemed undone on being discovered. Few people might criticize Mr. Wickham, but nearly everybody would blame Miss Derrythorpe for compromising her virtue. What words of rational understanding did the Beauty speak to herself after being found sitting astride her lover as if she were riding a horse?

All Anne knew is that by evening's end she herself had been thoroughly trampled, as much by Mr. Wickham's inconstancy as by Miss Derrythorpe's conniving character. It seemed their flirtation had been flowering for weeks, unbeknownst to anyone in the families. If true, their wiliness had been skillfully hidden from everybody. Which of them had led the chase? She could as easily picture Miss Derrythorpe's leadership as blame Wickham for his seduction. For all her beauty, Miss Derrythorpe possessed the character of a tomcat.

No, no, she told herself, I am not being fair. I must strive to be honest with myself.

If she criticized and scorned Miss Derrythorpe with such glee, what could be said for her own awful behavior with Mr. Wickham? She had loosed her animal spirits freely, believing them capable of regulation, only to hold no rein on their wild impulses. She had proved as stupid as Richardson's Pamela to have allowed herself to be maneuvered into an indelicate position. She had succumbed to charm and good looks, against her Papa's prediction, and now must address the question she had asked about Miss Waygood: Who feels most keenly the dishonor of untamed passion—her relations or herself?

Time was needed to recover from so idiotic and incomprehensible an episode. Discipline was needed to know herself.

She examined her crude sketch in the dim light. The root's stringy whiskers needed work, but she was too tired to continue. She blew out the candle and climbed into bed. It did no good to dwell on hurtful events. Within the next day or two she would have an opportunity to thank Fitzwilliam for coming to her aid. It was the least she could do, and it might help repair their relations.

Lord, she was tired as a haymaker.

Chapter 25

Effusions and Digressions

Several days passed in which Anne felt tired and disagreeable, her mind being seized with painful memories and forlorn hopes. She'd had no chance to thank Fitzwilliam for his kindness and quick thinking. And poor Mr. Derrythorpe. He must blame himself for failing to control his sister. But what could he have done? Miss Derrythorpe had followed her own advice. She had not appeared much interested in Mr. Wickham when they were in company together and thereby brought no undue attention to their flirtation. No one could have predicted her folly, which for all its awfulness, might have been far worse. Had Mr. Derrythorpe felt compelled to report his sister's bad behavior to Lord Matlock? Was the Beauty now in disgrace with her family? Would Mr. Wickham be punished?

Consideration of these intriguing questions was soon overcome by her mother's expressions of displeasure as Dawson maneuvered the de Bourgh coach through London's busy streets.

"I fail to understand why Mr. Newland could not be persuaded to move this appointment forward to next week," said

Lady Catherine. "It would be more convenient then, as we would be at our leisure. Today we had scheduled an appointment with Mr. Hoppner. We shall get quite soaked in this rain."

"Do not fret, my dear," soothed Sir Lewis. "Mr. Newland has only two documents to be signed. He will not claim more than a few minutes of our time, and the rain has lessened."

Lady Catherine had not finished fretting. "You know Mr. Newland. Our reputations will be quite ruined if we are late for Mr. Hoppner."

"All will be well," said Sir Lewis. "Our carriage shall stand out front, at hand for a ready departure, and Mr. Newland's office is not far from Charles Street. There will be ample time for our timely arrival at Mr. Hoppner's, I assure you."

"You may assure all you please, but Mr. Newland has shown himself to be exceedingly inflexible," said Lady Catherine, determined to have the last word.

Anne was relieved by her father's calmness of temper, which had the happy capacity of moderating her mother's flutterings without insulting her feelings. Would that she, his daughter, could learn from his example. How had he become so adept? Was his sensibility innate, formed at birth, the tendency trained by his mother when he was but a child? Or had he acquired this understanding as his marriage matured? Perhaps like an admiral of the Royal Navy, Papa chose his battles carefully.

She studied him in the light filtered through the carriage window. Worn by weather and time, his was still a handsome face, possessed of deep-set, hazel-hued eyes sheltered by ragged eyebrows turning gray. His hair was a little long and wild, which fact never pleased her mother, but his features were strong and manly, proclaiming his character: he was not easily fooled or challenged, as she well knew.

At the moment he did not seem quite himself, for his usual style was to allow his wife the privilege of thinking her words ended the discussion, only to insert a retort a few minutes later that provoked her in some frivolous way. Anne could imagine his saying, "If we find ourselves short of time, my love, we shall leave the carriage in Dawson's faithful hands and run on foot to Mr. Hoppner's. In that way, we arrive on time, if disordered, soaked to the skin, and out of breath." That he made no such comment was surprising, but he looked preoccupied and likely thought it prudent to keep his breath to cool his porridge.

The gentleman whose behavior peeved Lady Catherine was a respectable solicitor who had served the de Bourgh family for many years. On arriving at his office near Lincoln's Inn, the amanuensis ushered the de Bourghs into a small sitting room and pulled the door closed behind him.

Lady Catherine sank onto the Chippendale sofa, annoyed with her husband for allowing Mr. Newland's discourtesy. Sir Lewis, knowing better than to stir his wife's ill temper, took an elbow-chair near the window, picked up a recent issue of *The London Magazine*, and gave it a desultory look. Anne moved behind the sofa to investigate the leather-bound books that lined the floor-to-ceiling cases. The rich Oriental rug underfoot and tiled fireplace fronted by two brass iron dogs bespoke comfort and decorum.

A few minutes later, Mr. Josiah Newland stepped into the room. Following close on his heels was a young man who could only be his son, their likeness being quite similar.

Mr. Newland opened with great civility. "Lady Catherine, please allow me to say how well you look." He took her gloved hand briefly. "Are you enjoying your residence in Town? Have you circulated to the Theatre Royal or taken in a play in Drury Lane? Do you stay for the season to enjoy the balls at Almack's? Surely, you cannot deny your lovely daughter a chance to dance at Almack's! It is every girl's heart's desire." He glanced at Anne as if in conspiracy with her before rushing on. "Her enchanting figure will charm many a young man and bring much approbation to your family. You would not wish to deny her a lifetime of happy memories, I am sure you would not. And you, yourself, must enjoy a little dancing. Ah, do not frown, for I can imagine your dancing at a masquerade ball disguised as Helen of Troy or a muse—Clio, perhaps, or Calliope."

He waggled a finger at her, barked a high laugh, and patted his liver, seemingly pleased this formality was behind him, and shifted his welcome to Sir Lewis, leaving a grim smile fixed to Lady Catherine's face.

"Sir Lewis, it is good to see you again," he said, giving a curt bow. "I appreciate your flexibility in following through on my small request for a change in date. Your kindness has allowed me to travel north to visit my mother a day earlier. Were it not for good clients like you, I would be quite done in, I'm sure. Few clients would—"

"My pleasure, Mr. Newland," Sir Lewis cut in, taking care not to look at his wife, who was quite put out on hearing that her precious schedule had been modified to accommodate Mr. Newland's mother. "You seem well."

"I am, thank you. Only a few gouty twinges linger in this disagreeable weather ..."

Throughout these exchanges, Anne stood riveted behind the sofa. Papa had warned her the gentleman could be eccentric. She had been prepared for eccentricity of dress. Her mind's image of the solicitor had not been far off the mark, for Mr. Newland was stylishly but uncomfortably clothed. His white cravat was tied too tightly, the stricture reddening his face with the exertion of his labored breathing, and his blue waistcoat was ill-fitting. It stretched so severely across his middle that Anne feared a button would pop off and fly across the room if he but sneezed or coughed during one of his speeches.

As for his personality, she had failed completely in her prediction. He was nothing like Hunsford's elderly solicitor, Mr. Cobb, who stalked about the village clad always in black, reminding one of a stark crow searching for litter in the hedgerows. Where Mr. Cobb was always formal, even officious, Mr. Newland was spirited in form and casual in conversation; his effusions and digressions flowed naturally from some deep well of inspiration.

How interesting that he should support her own claim for permission to dance at Almack's, assuming, of course, she could obtain a voucher. But the look on Mama's face when he proposed her dressing as Clio or Calliope at a masked ball—it was too delicious!

"Let me introduce my daughter, Anne," Sir Lewis said. He swept an arm in her direction.

At this invitation, Anne skirted the sofa to offer a formal curtsy to Mr. Newland, who stepped forward, shook her hand, and studied her face. He chattered pleasantly about how petite and pretty she was and how she favored her father. Such personal comments might have embarrassed her had they come from any other strange man, but Anne could not take offense at Mr. Newland's style, for he seemed the very pillar of sincerity. Indeed, she could have listened to him for hours, so enraptured was she by his free-hearted speech.

After declaring her presentation at court the next year would be a great success, he said, "Allow me to introduce my son Cleveland, who joined my company this year."

Mr. Cleveland Newland bowed to each of them in turn. His manner was not so exuberant as his father's, causing Anne to wonder whether his quiet demeanor was for show or a reflection of his true nature. Given the unpredictable directions of his father's improvisations, a calm façade was likely the only appropriate choice in company. Was he embarrassed by his father's giddy performance or, if not embarrassed, at least a little piqued by it? His countenance betrayed no resentment. Rather, he seemed to enjoy his father's discourse. After the elder Mr. Newland invited her father down the hall to his private office, still talking of Anne's many charms, she had the opportunity of taking the son's measure.

Mr. Cleveland Newland pulled the elbow-chair closer to the fireplace. Anne took a seat on the sofa near her mother. For a moment they sat in silence, listening to the amanuensis rustle books and papers in the outer room. Through the open door, they heard his chair creak when he sat down.

"Do you enjoy being in Town, Miss de Bourgh?" asked Mr. Cleveland Newland.

"Oh, yes. It offers many diversions, but I enjoy it best in small doses. I would become quite mad if I lived always within its environs. I cannot bear to be too long away from Rosings." Anne surprised herself by speaking so frankly.

"Your point is well taken. Many people find its entertainments exhausting," he replied. "For myself, I can imagine living no other place. I would miss the coffee houses and clubs and exhibits. In London I exist in a near perpetual state of excitement." A smile lit his face as if he were a child given a new toy.

"You are an intellectual, then, like Dr. Johnson, who claimed that when a man is tired of London, he is tired of life."

"You have pegged me exactly. I seldom wander much farther from Town than Northamptonshire, where I go to visit my grandmother, but I would like to see Kent one day. I hear it is beautiful—the Garden of England. If I could forbear the thousand dissipations of London, Kent might be the perfect place to live."

"You cannot praise Kent too highly for my taste," Anne told him, "but I believe your opportunities would be severely constrained. Our village of Hunsford has one solicitor who serves a few hundred town folks. Here, there are thousands of interesting people from which to draw your clients."

"You are right there," he said. "Our clients are mostly land-owners with seats in the country and residences in London. If there is a demarcation among them, it is not usually one of earl versus viscount or baronet, but of Tory versus Whig."

"Really? I had not realized the legal profession was divided so strictly along political lines."

"Isn't everything?" he challenged, one eyebrow raised.

"I suppose you are right," said Anne, not caring to admit her lack of thought on the matter, beyond knowing her parents were devout Tories.

"But the dividing line is less fixed today than in previous generations," Mr. Newland continued, "for we serve commerce, and commerce knows no political boundaries."

"May I ask, Mr. Newland, if you would not think me too inquisitive, how you came to be drawn to the law as a profession?"

Even though she felt strangely tired and cross, Anne shoul-dered the burden of polite conversation while her mother sat statue-like, staring past Mr. Newland's head to the heavily draped window beyond.

"Your question is not impertinent. I was drawn initially to the Church and imagined myself serving my fellow man as a vicar. I would write sermons, corral the wayward, inspire the wicked to repent, and organize charities for the unfortunates. I sought to serve God through good works. My father had no objection to my entering the clergy, but he encouraged me to consider the law, believing my character well suited for it. While I was at Cambridge, my tutor, Mr. Adam Lorne—a fine man of good fortune—inspired me to examine my father's profession with greater objectivity than I had been wont to do. In the end, I chose the law, thus making my father happy."

Anne could not blame him for basking with such visible pleasure in the approval of his father.

"The brass plate on the front door denotes the firm's functions as 'solicitors' and 'conveyancers.' Do you serve in one capacity or the other?"

"I am a solicitor studying the art and science of conveyancing."

Anne suspected he toyed with her, but she did not mind. "I fear I am not much enlightened by your answer. What, precisely, is conveyancing? Surely it has nothing to do with transporting cabbages and rutabagas!"

Mr. Newland laughed at her ignorance. "No, conveyancing deals with the buying and selling of real property, by which I mean land and buildings. It is an endeavor requiring considerable attention to detail and precedent."

While thinking about his earnest answer and its possible connection with her father's appointment, Anne studied his person. He had a pale complexion and plump cheeks. She wondered how this small, sturdy man could seem overly large in the cozy sitting room. In return, his bright eyes gazed at her with a direct but not provoking certainty, making her feel as if she were the only object of his endeavors for the morning— indeed, as if she were the only lady in all of Holborn. Her admiration for Mr. Cleveland, as she came to think of him, advanced in direct proportion to the intensity of his regard.

She glanced at her mother, sitting like a statue, and marveled that her ladyship made no move to direct the conversation. Believing she should at least display a little good breeding, Anne plowed onward, saying, "My father has spoken of your company's success. I had no idea the buying and selling of property afforded such steady business."

"Oh, yes. It is highly lucrative. Every landowner needs a conveyancer to protect his—or her—property. Our clients are diverse in their characters and whims but steady in their needs.

You will be much amused by the case of Mr. Fairley-Evans Hogsmouth," he said, as if to prove how diverse his client's characters could be. "You may have read of his exploits in the broadsides. An intelligent man born into wealth, Mr. Hogsmouth maintained a comfortable seat for his wife and children in the country. How did he spend his time as a gentleman, one might ask? Did he fish or run his hounds? Was he a literary gentleman with a fine library? Did he study rocks and trees? No! He roamed London as a mumper. A mumper! Can you imagine? He preferred to work disguised as a woman—one day, a filthy gypsy; the next day, a castoff consumptive. Any disguise would do so long as it enriched his purse. His success as a beggar earned him considerable esteem in some parts of Town. Even his parents and neighbors failed to recognize his disguised person."

"How extraordinary. Are you prepared to acknowledge his political affiliation?"

"He was a Tory from head to toe." Mr. Newland grinned.

"But why would he need your services? Has he been gaoled?"

"Oh, no. He is dead," lamented Mr. Newland, as if death had no right to claim such an imaginative man. "Occasionally, however, his heir requires our assistance writing mortgages and transferring property."

"I daresay many of your cases are not so interesting."

"That is true, but the monotony of a dull case is often superseded by the ridiculousness of the client."

Anne laughed at his frank confession. She had been on the point of inquiring where he placed her family on his scale of the absurd when the amanuensis arrived to announce the completion of her father's business. She was sorry for the interruption, for she was fairly sure Mr. Cleveland would answer her question truthfully, without regard for any delicate sensibilities on her side.

On the drive to Mr. Hoppner's studio in Mayfair, Lady Catherine made no mention of Mr. Cleveland Newland, as if they had never been introduced, as if she had not endured twenty minutes listening to his conversation. Instead, she proclaimed his father, Mr. Josiah Newland, worthy of every criticism related to his ludicrous dress and manners. She named each affront to her person, marveled at his presumptions—why, she would sooner disport in Bath's public springs than attend a masked ball dressed as a Greek muse—and petitioned her husband for a more sympathetic legal advisor.

Sir Lewis listened and nodded his understanding of her wishes.

Anne kept an eye on the London foot traffic and ignored her mother's pleadings. For her, the young Mr. Cleveland's vibrant personality was a source of steady contemplation. To status and rank, he appeared oblivious, but that was not surprising, as his father served many peers of the realm. As to looks, he was very like his father in appearance, being short and stout with fair, sparse hair that covered his crown like duck down. Although his physical attributes did little to recommend him as a romantic interest, his manners were delightfully comic. All told, he had been cordial but not overly deferential.

What would it be like to be married to such a man? Would his character be a continual source of amusement, or would it be wearing? Frankly, she could not imagine life as Mrs. Cleveland Newland, but then she couldn't image life as Mrs. Fitzwilliam Darcy either. Even so, she admired his ready intelligence and easy manner and marveled that a man whose appearance was anything but manly should be so forceful and confident.

They arrived at Mr. Hoppner's on time, their reputations intact. Mr. John Hoppner proved less entertaining than Mr. Cleveland Newland, by way of his being older and more sophisticated and, therefore, less interesting as a person.

Sir Lewis appeared little impressed with Mr. Hoppner's reputation and connections, for he scribbled notes in a small pocketbook while the artist praised his own talent. Anne observed her mother, who softened under Mr. Hoppner's gallant manners and flattery, smiled pleasantly, and nodded her agreement as he described his proposed course for painting Miss de Bourgh's portrait.

Anne appreciated his wit but was offended by his deference to her mother. After all, it was her portrait, not her mother's, being commissioned. But she could not be disagreeable for long, as Mr. Hoppner's studio contained several nearly finished portraits of young ladies, to which she was drawn for the study of his technique. In short order, her parents agreed to return in six weeks for Anne's first sitting, the family leaving with Mr. Hoppner's assurance of rendering a memorable likeness of their lovely daughter.

Chapter 26

Thunderbolts

"You look as if you ate a sour apple pudding for breakfast," Miss Waygood told Anne as she pulled on her gloves. "Shall I retrieve Dr. Buchan's book from the library? It might offer a cure for your sallow complexion and bad temper." Her eyes raked Anne's dress from head to toe. "You cannot wear that pelisse. There is quite a strong wind this morning, which rattled the attic window in my room and kept me awake most of the night."

Ignoring Anne's scowl, she turned to the butler. "Juggins, will you find Miss de Bourgh's brown pelisse? Dobbie knows where it is."

"Yes, ma'am." Juggins did not look as though he cared for the effort, but he climbed the stairs none the less, leaving the young ladies standing in the entrance hall.

"Isabelle, you shouldn't ask him to run errands. His rheumatism is bothering him this morning, poor man. Could you not detect his discomfort?" Anne had no patience for teasing this morning—she'd never heard of a sour apple pudding; there were baked apple puddings and carrot, rice, and marrow puddings, and Damson puddings (her favorite), but not sour apple puddings—nor had she any interest in retrieving the good doctor's book *Domestic Medicine*, nor did she hold with pestering a faithful servant who wasn't feeling well. She merely wanted to get on with the day. "I can do very well with this pelisse. It's windy, true enough, but it's no howling gale. I'm not likely to be carried aloft across the river to Greenwich, and our journey is not far."

"Juggins did not object to my small request. He likes to be useful."

"Lady Catherine also likes to be useful, but I haven't known you to make small requests of her."

Five minutes later a frowning governess accompanied her scowling charge into the street. Although she would never admit it, Anne was grateful for her brown pelisse. The wind grabbed at her ankles, whipped her gown's hem, and buffeted her bonnet as she marched east with Miss Waygood. Their journey along Russell Street was hardly more than a stone's throw from Bedford Square, but both travelers sighed their relief on being admitted to the British Museum at the designated time. Their wait for the Derrythorpes in the reception saloon was not long.

"Good Lord!" cried Miss Derrythorpe before even offering her well-wishes. "The wind is a tornado today. My eyes are full of grit. You look completely done in, Miss de Bourgh, and you have walked a mere two blocks. We braved the gusts on foot all the way from St. James's Square."

"Then you are to be congratulated for your fortitude," Anne replied.

Seeing which way the wind blew, Miss Waygood took Mr. Derrythorpe's arm, saying, "I have been pondering which artifacts might be most pleasing to you. I suggest we find the Egyptian antiquities. I believe they are along this corridor at the back of the building, and you'll want to see the Magna Carta. This way if you please." She pulled Mr. Derrythorpe across the room, leaving Anne and Miss Derrythorpe standing under the painted, domed ceiling where Jupiter flung his thunderbolts at Phaeton.

"Does your governess always put herself forward so boldly?" asked Miss Derrythorpe. "The last governess I had, Miss Thomson, nearly fainted if anyone other than family spoke to her. She would never separate a young man whom she barely knew from his companions and draw him off to some remote room."

"Miss Waygood is quite amiable and perfectly trustworthy. She likely feels she knows your brother sufficiently well to be comfortable in his company. After all, she and I spent a morning with him at St. Paul's Cathedral. That was shortly after you fainted at the Lion's Tower, you may recall, and he *should* view the Egyptian artifacts. They are magnificent."

Miss Derrythorpe's eyes glinted. "I recall him saying that Miss Waygood disappeared for some time that day, which gave him the opportunity of viewing the nave and galleries alone with you."

"Yes, well, she left briefly to retrieve a pair of gloves she had purchased. Is there anything you'd like to view? I can recommend the Athenian vases—they are a vivid red and black, nothing like what we use today—and the Etruscan vases and statuary are remarkable. You have only to tell me what you wish to see." Here, Anne began walking toward the stairs. Miss Derrythorpe trailed along beside her, not the least interested in anything the great museum might offer.

Anne's patience had never been so sorely tested, for Miss Derrythorpe took no pleasure in anything. The Beauty stood briefly looking down into a glass case of ancient coins before flitting off to examine Sir Hans Sloane's 20,000 medals, all arranged in narrow cabinets, which captured her fancy for perhaps a minute. When Anne admired the mythical, god-like creatures painted on a large Etruscan water jug, Miss Derry-thorpe said, "They are obscene. Why would a winged camel have four teats? It isn't natural." When invited to examine an especially striking set of figures engraved on an ancient Greek amphora, she merely glanced at it, snorting, "Humph," before wandering into an adjacent room.

In the room housing the Pompeii and Herculaneum arti-facts, Anne's pleasure was overshadowed by her companion's flirtation with a man old enough to be her grandfather. The gentleman was well-dressed, if a little portly, and carried a cane, but his person appeared somewhat unkempt: his generous beard, flecked with gray, seemed never to have been trimmed, while his snowy white curls flung themselves in odd directions about his ears. He clearly relished these few minutes engaged with a new and very pretty acquaintance, smiling down on her like an indulgent grandpapa. Anne watched them examining a cabinet containing gold jewelry and short statues unearthed at the archaeologic sites. He made a joke that brought forth a loud laugh from Miss Derrythorpe. Several patrons turned in their direction. At first Anne was determined to ignore them, but when she saw the man take Miss Derrythorpe's elbow in an overly friendly manner, she decided it was time to intervene.

"Excuse me, sir, but my companion and I must be careful of the time. Shall we find your brother?" she said, looking at Miss Derrythorpe.

"Of course, I must not keep you," he said graciously. If he was surprised to learn the young lady had a companion nearby, he did not show it. "Thank you for entertaining me." He bowed to Miss Derrythorpe and disappeared into another room.

"You had no right to interfere. We were having a per-fectly amiable conversation about fashion. He has returned to England after several years living in France and was most humorous in describing the differences in our gowns and hair styles." Miss Derrythorpe looked askance at Anne. "Our conversation was none of your business in any event. You have become quite a busybody in recent days."

Anne pulled the Beauty into a corner, having had her fill of insolence. "What do you mean? You seem content to make clear that you are peeved with me without having the courtesy to tell me why. I want to know."

"Well, if you're going to be so snippy I will tell you that I do not appreciate your telling my aunt about my secret meeting with Mr. Wickham at Sir Robert's ball. Oh, the threats and torments I've endured. At one point my uncle vowed to lock me in my bedchamber, while my aunt lectured me about prudence and purity. As a result of your meddling, I've been banned from doing just about everything but accompanying my brother or one of my cousins on their errands. It is too much. Do not pretend it wasn't you."

Anne inhaled a deep breath. "I did not do it."

"You must think me a simpleton. I know you spoke with my aunt when she called on Lady Catherine last week. She mentioned visiting with you briefly."

"That much is true. Papa and I were preparing to walk to Hookham's circulating library, and while we waited for our coats we greeted aunt Fitzwilliam in the drawing room. We spoke only common pleasantries. Nothing more. Even had there been an opportunity to speak privately with her, I would not have shared with her any information about you and Mr. Wickham."

"Why should I believe you? You are plain and common and resent the fact that Mr. Wickham chose me over yourself. It is often the way, I find."

Anne studied Miss Derrythorpe's kittenish face, so sweet, so fairy-like in shadow. Her delicate features hid a calculating and petty mind; her pretty hands were as sharply clawed as a tiger's. I hope none of my cousins marry her or her like, she said to herself.

"It is truly unfair to speak so," Anne said softly, "for I know very well my own deficiencies. But where Mr. Wickham is concerned I did not—would not—tell our aunt of your meeting him in secret, for I have as much to be ashamed of as you." She was pleased to see her companion's surprised look. "You do not know?"

"I am ashamed of nothing. As for you—you are in love with him and flatter yourself that he returns your affection. What else is there?"

Anne steadied herself, not feeling confident about the wisdom of making a confession. "You remember the dinner and dance my family hosted a few weeks ago? I was caught with Mr. Wickham in our townhouse library that evening. My father and Mr. Darcy came upon us while we sat in the dark … in an intimate embrace. How I wish I could return to that moment and make a different decision! But what is done, is done." She touched Miss Derrythorpe's arm briefly. "Do you understand? It would be monstrous of me to criticize you when I am guilty of the same offense. Shame prevented me from telling aunt Fitzwilliam about your tryst with Mr. Wickham."

"So you say," said Miss Derrythorpe, thrusting her nose in the air before prancing down the corridor, leaving Anne to wonder whether she had made matters better or worse.

Chapter 27

Offending Humors

"Why are you not dressed this morning?"

Lady Catherine's voice rang loudly as she strode about Anne's bedchamber, lifting books and opening cabinet drawers. Leaning over her daughter's worktable like a general studying a battle plan, she surveyed the drawing tablets, watercolors, brushes and crayons, the dried acorns, twigs, and pressed maple leaves. Two volumes of *Curtis's Botanical Magazine* lay across a chipped delftware platter and had likely been pilfered from Sir Lewis's library. A reddish, shriveled root caught her eye, its purpose being unfathomable until she spied its rustic likeness on paper. Moving to the dressing table, she searched through the stationery, most of which was blank, and finding nothing to please her, picked up a note in Tilly's handwriting, which she read straight through, her lips moving, before throwing it to the floor. Next she found a letter Anne had addressed to Tilly the day before Sir Robert's ball. The letter's few sentences contained no personal reflections, but merely inquired about Tilly's trip to Sevenoaks with her father. This, too, was tossed on the floor.

Anne pushed back the bed cover and struggled to a sitting position. What was her mother doing?

Dobbie stood speechless as Lady Catherine read Anne's letter. Under what pretense could her ladyship justify invading her daughter's privacy? Gracious heaven, Anne was still a child, but even so, she deserved some measure of respect for her private affairs, however inconsequential they might seem to her mother.

"Lady Catherine, have you misplaced something? May I help search for it?" Dobbie's nerves were all ajar for fear she would be forced to hand over the paisley shawl.

Lady Catherine gave no hint that she had heard Dobbie's offer but rounded on Anne. "Get dressed immediately and join me in the drawing room."

"Lady Catherine, if you please," said Dobbie, "you should know—"

This was said to Lady Catherine's back as she swept from the room and pulled the solid door closed behind her.

"Well, I never." Dobbie turned to help Anne prepare for her summons. "I would prefer you stay in bed. I am sure you have a fever, and your color is high. We must send for Mr. Hawkabee. He is such a good soul and gave your father every attention last year when he had so many mysterious aches. You remember that time and how Mr. Hawkabee arrived in a heavy rain ..." As she helped Anne dress, Dobbie's mutterings mingled her thoughts about surgeons, fevers, and bloodletting with observations on Sir Lewis's illness, Lady Catherine's unexpected demands, and the sad lot of old servants.

Downstairs Anne paused in the hall, feeling light-headed but not daring to rest a minute on one of the hall chairs. Hearing voices, she proceeded to the drawing room where a liveried servant opened the door for her. When she advanced into the room, she was surprised to see Mr. and Mrs. Dighurst.

"Tell us what you know about Miss Waygood and Mr. Dighurst," demanded Lady Catherine.

Anne looked blankly at her mother.

"Lady Catherine, give her time to collect herself," said Mrs. Dighurst, whose comportment betrayed her anxiety. "Miss de Bourgh, you and Miss Waygood are friends. Did she speak to you of having a particular regard for my son?"

"No, ma'am," Anne replied, "she never said any such thing." This, at least, was a true statement.

Mr. Dighurst stood rigidly next to the sofa. A ferocious glower supplanted his normally congenial demeanor. He could not keep silent. "She never mentioned a plan to elope with him?"

"No! Has she eloped?" Anne was bewildered by the direction of this conversation, for Isabelle had as good as denied any intimacy with Mr. Dighurst. Had Isabelle held a greater affection for their Hunsford neighbor than Anne had heretofore suspected? Perhaps Isabelle and Mr. Dighurst had agreed to elope that day when Mr. Derrythorpe spied the two of them in the street from the outdoor gallery atop St. Paul's.

Lady Catherine's patience wore thin. "Did Miss Waygood leave a letter for you? Did she write you of a plan to elope with Mr. Dighurst? Come, girl, do not stand there like a blockhead. Speak!"

"No, I—I—" Anne stammered as the sound of a rushing river filled her ears. The room began to revolve, the swirling motion making her quite dizzy. *Good God, I am going to faint.*

She slumped in a heap on the wool rug, a loud, persistent ringing in her ears. Her mother stood nearby, thrusting her arms in first one direction and then another; her shouted commands were mute to Anne's ear. Mrs. Dighurst knelt by her side and rubbed her hand, her lips moving in silent appeal. Mr. Dighurst stood behind his wife, a worried crease on his brow.

Anne felt queasy and disoriented. Someone lifted her, clumsily, the effort crushing her gown. Ah, Papa. She smelled his clothes and felt his strong arms as she was carried up the stairs, after which time was lost.

Later Anne woke to muffled voices. She lay in bed in a darkened room. A fire had been laid and her bed moved closer to the hearth to receive its warmth. She felt no need of blankets or clothes, for her body was aflame. Time and again she pushed back the heavy quilt to cool her animal heat, but in every instance someone—"Dobbie, is that you?"—spoke soothing words, tucked in her arms, and pulled the cover up over her chest.

In the flickering light, she recognized Mr. Hawkabee, his curly beard puffed out like a strange bird's nest sitting on the end of his chin. His brow wrinkled as he spoke with someone in the shadows.

"Her temperature is volatile. Therefore we must invigorate the sweating to cast out the subtile matter. I advise cupping, to draw the heat from her body. Let her maid apply hot compresses afterward."

The conversation drifted in soft syllables. Her nightgown was removed, and her body rolled over to expose her bare back. (Oh, blessed relief to feel cool air upon her blistering skin.) Next a searing heat scorched the skin along her spine, causing her to cry out in surprise and pain. This first shock was followed by another and still another, each singe a torture. Her arms were pinned down and, again, came the hot cup, the singeing pain. She whimpered. The once calm voice trembled.

How many days passed she could not say. At first her throat was on fire, the pain of swallowing such an agony she refused to eat or drink.

Whenever she sensed Mr. Hawkabee's presence, she struggled to concentrate, for his discussion of physic would interest her, but the effort to comprehend his fragmented instructions was great.

"It is a putrid fever. The offending humors must be cast out."

The fog of fever prevented her hearing the hushed conversation until the doctor approached her bedside and touched her face. "Give her a draught of Dover's Powder to stimulate sweating."

"Shall you try bloodletting?" Papa's strained voice came from the shadows.

"Yes, I shall bleed her, but Dover's mix of ipecacuanha and opium will also do some good. If her fever does not break, a more assertive regimen can be tried later. Antimony might work to purge the bowels. The putrefaction must not be allowed to stagnate."

Purge … putrefaction … her senses succumbed to fever and fretfulness. Many days were lost in a miserable stupor while her body was besieged with sweats and fevers.

Chapter 28

Almost Supernatural

Anne awoke to the familiar sound of a broom sweeping hearth stone. Under heavy lids she spied first the red drapes, which had been parted a mere hand's length to give Betsy sufficient light to clean the bricks and lay coal. Next the high-backed chair came into focus; a newly ironed bed-sheet had been thrown over its shoulder like a shroud. Closer at hand were two small tables strewn with half-melted candles; a tinder-box; several dark brown bottles bearing the apothecary's label; a crumpled lace handkerchief; a small porcelain bowl; and something unfamiliar—what were these?—pine-cones. How odd. When Betsy stood, her task finished, Anne closed her eyes and sank again into sleep.

Mid-morning she stirred. Dobbie stood at the foot of the bed, holding two chemises to the meagre window light, the drapes having now been thrown open.

The pearly rays filtered through low clouds reminded Anne of Rosings. She pictured herself there, standing in her little garden on a cloudy day. Not one to shy from farm work, she had convinced Cook to give her a patch of ground in the kitchen garden. Always keen to indulge the child, no matter what her ladyship said, Cook began to teach her everything she knew about growing vegetables and fruit. That first year of gardening was no great success in terms of bounty, but it pleased the eight-year-old Anne. With each passing spring she grew more accomplished, such that a decade later Cook gladly told everybody the truth: "Miss Anne grows the best strawberries of any farmer for miles around." The previous summer her blackcurrants and peas had been exceptional. Might she do as well this year? She hoped for the strength to redesign her flower garden and check her seeds and bulbs.

"Dobbie, what day is it?"

"Goodness, child! You fair startled me." Dobbie laid down the laundry and set to plumping Anne's pillows and straightening the bed-sheets. "You've been abed for more than three weeks, love. Today is the eighth of January and right cloudy and cold it is. We shall have rain tomorrow for sure."

"Am I recovered?"

Dobbie looked down on her young charge with a mother's kind eyes. "You had an awfully feverish infection and we feared we might lose you a night or two. But Dr. Hawkabee took charge, got you over the rough patches, and says you'll soon be fit as a fiddle. All you need is rest and good food."

Anne felt decidedly foggy. "When do we return to Rosings?"

"No decision has been made. We must first put som' meat on your bones, else you freeze solid on the trip home. Beef broth will do for lunch. You must be sick t' death of barley water an' lemonade." Dobbie crossed her arms over her ample bosom. "Would you like to sit before the fire? I can make it nice an' cozy in here. Would you like that?"

"I would."

"Your father will be very glad to hear it, for he has been worryin' mightily during these weeks when you've been so ill."

"Where did the pine-cones come from? I don't recall gathering them."

Dobbie chuckled. "They are a gift, one might say, from Mr. Derrythorpe. He and his sister and your cousin—Mr. Fitzwilliam, the younger, of whom you are so fond—called on you the day after you were taken ill. Miss Derrythorpe, being such a thoughtful and sweet mannered child, brought you a jar of quince marmalade, which you can have a bite of tomorrow, but Mr. Derrythorpe carried those very pine-cones, sayin' he knew you'd want to draw them. Well, her ladyship, no surprise to you or anybody else, saw no reason for givin' you worthless pine-cones, and so she summoned Betsy to do away with them after your guests left the house. I happen'd to be in the kitchen when Betsy brought them down and figured I'd bring 'em up here, considerin' how kind Mr. Derrythorpe had been to think of you."

"Yes, so kind. Are they still in Town?"

"I heard they left the very next day, travelin' to Clun for Christmas. The Darcys left Town a few days later, not that they wanted to, mind you. They were all for stayin' here—includin' young Mr. Darcy, I'll have you know—until your health was assured, but your papa convinced them to return to Derbyshire. There was nothing more to be done for you, and all we could do was wait for your fever to break, which it did, thank the good Lord."

Under no circumstances would she mention Mr. Wickham, who had accompanied the Darcys to Pemberley. Nothing good would come of getting Miss Anne riled up about him. Nor would she discuss the Dighursts, who had returned, heavy hearted, to Hunsford after failing to obtain any news of their son and Miss Waygood.

"Lady Matlock and your cousins long ago returned to Wiltshire," Dobbie added, "but Lord Matlock stayed in Town. He would not depart until he heard you were on the mend, but he left last week to attend to his estate while the weather is agreeable."

"And what of Miss Waygood? Is she well?"

"You are not to concern yourself with her now. You must rest an' recover." Dobbie's tone did not invite more questions.

Over the next days Anne gained strength to be dressed and sit before the fire. Her appetite returned, to Dobbie's high praises. She was not allowed to come downstairs for meals or company and so amused herself by reading or listening to Dobbie's chatter or watching the house maids change the bed-sheets.

One glorious morning, when she longed to be out in the square or walking along Piccadilly, she sought solace in drawing. It felt like months since she had last been lost to time by sketching. How pleasant to return to it. With some effort, for she tired easily and must steady herself by holding onto the furniture, she fetched her favorite sketch book and tin of crayons. For a subject, she chose a pretty plate on which Mrs. Juggins had placed two small scones and a petite cup of jam. With her chair situated near the fireplace, a blanket thrown across her legs, and Isabelle's shawl wrapped around her shoulders, she settled herself next to a small table on which was positioned the delftware plate and its scones.

She balanced the sketch book on her lap and browsed the first few pages. Here was her portrait of Tilly dressed in a blue-dotted muslin gown trimmed with yellow ribbons; her lips were pressed in a firm line, her profile a study in concentration. Next came a sketch of Mr. Sullen's muddy boots. (Nicely done—a solid likeness, Anne thought.) That day, she and Tilly had planned to walk to the mantua-maker's shop, but a sudden storm forced them indoors. They were obliged to keep their voices low so as not to disturb Tilly's father as he worked on his sermon. He kept the study door partially closed, which was just as well, for had he been aware of their intent, he would not have approved of their bringing his boots into the parlor and placing them on the hearth where the light was good.

The next few pages were simple sketches of oak trees, mushrooms, and apples.

On leafing to the first blank page, Anne found a sheaf of paper laid face-side down. Turning it over, she recognized Isabelle's handwriting. A date of December 16th appeared at the top of the page in bold cursive.

> *Dearest Anne,*
>
> *By the time you read this letter, I will have left your household to establish my own. You, Clever Girl, have long suspected an affection between myself and dear Mr. Dighurst. We wish we could share our joy with you, but you can imagine our need for secrecy. Do not think us reckless, for we have given much thought and prayer to this chosen path. I will write when we are settled and only hope my letter reaches you directly. Know that I hold you in my heart and call you My Own Sweet Friend.*
>
> *Yours in true affection, Isabelle*

Isabelle and Mr. Dighurst had eloped! The lovers had departed their former lives together, married quietly, and formed their own household. Would they have left London? Isabelle once expressed delight in the seashore. Did they go to Brighton? Had they been discovered? Perhaps they had returned to Bardolph Hall. How thrilling it would be to have her friend living close by. Was that why Isabelle had given her the paisley shawl? She knew she would be leaving the de Bourghs' employ and wished to leave a memento with her young companion. How like Isabelle to think of her at such a moment.

The more Anne pondered Isabelle's treasured letter, the more excited she became to return to Rosings. She must build her strength, for she now had every expectation of a happy home-coming. When her energy returned she would write Tilly for news.

She leaned against the pillows and reread Isabelle's letter several times before returning it to its hiding place. As she drowsed before the fire, her thoughts were filled with pleasant images of her homecoming and Isabelle's warm welcome. Their friendship must change now that Isabelle was married, but she had no fear of rejection. Isabelle was her own sweet friend and Mr. Dighurst had ever been kind to her. She felt something very like true contentment before nodding off to sleep.

She woke to the sound of Dobbie retrieving the china plate and jam cup.

"Did I wake you? It's just as well if I did, for I want you to drink this white caudle, which I brewed for you myself," she said as she placed a caudle cup on the small table. "Sir Lewis is hoping you will be well enough to come downstairs for dinner tomorrow. It would please him no end. I shall ask Cook to make a trifle, that being your favorite dessert, and you shall have some roast beef. It's time you took regular meals. After all, a good beginning makes a good ending."

Anne nodded and sipped from the two-handled cup while Dobbie bustled about, chattering about the weather and the price of coal and Betsy's bunions. "She's much too young to be bothered with sore feet. If she had listened to me—"

Anne felt as if she had come to wake on a broad beach after surviving a tempest-tossed voyage. This familiar china cup warming her hands was her talisman, her link with a past life, hazily remembered. Perhaps it was learning from Dobbie that she had nearly died, or hearing that Papa was so distraught he did not eat for days while her fever raged, or maybe it was the simple pleasure of sitting before the fire, of believing she would return to her former self, that accounted for her feeling remarkably serene.

A great bubble of happiness broke over her as she watched Dobbie busy herself counting handkerchiefs and stockings. Soon she would return to the comfort and beauty of Rosings where she would find joy in Tilly's company and renew her friendship with Isabelle. She felt untroubled by her engagement to Fizwilliam. She harbored no resentment toward Miss Derrythorpe. Her heart no longer ached for Mr. Wickham. Her one kernel of regret was that she had not said good-bye to Mr. Derrythorpe, whom she counted a friend. Much work lay ahead: she must learn to govern her heart, control her passions, and figure out what sort of character she desired in a husband—he would not be Fitzwilliam, not if she found the wherewithal to control her future—but these were matters to reflect on when her strength returned.

All the world this morning seemed oddly new and foreign. How strange and disconcerting to feel somehow different, almost supernatural, as if she had been turned on a bright heavenly wheel or whirled by an unseen force—perhaps magic or gravity or electricity.

Dobbie's dear voice came to her. "Wouldn't you agree, love?"

Anne drank up her maid's twinkling eyes and ruddy cheeks. She had no idea what Dobbie's question referred to, but she readily replied: "Yes. Yes, I would."

They smiled at each other like cherubs clutching rainbows.

###

Acknowledgements

Many people provided support during the writing, editing, and publishing of this novel. My younger brother, Steve, never failed to ask about my progress and how many books I sold; he is one of my most stalwart and enthusiastic supporters. Thanks, brother! Several dear friends called or emailed me to say how much they enjoyed my first novel, *Rosings Park*. Their interest and kind words sustained me. Peter, my dear husband, reminds me often of how important it is to pursue an activity I value, especially during those times when I wonder what the heck I'm doing. And he's a good sport: he helped me complete all eight Regency walks listed in Louise Allen's excellent book, *Walking Jane Austen's London*. He never complained and took more than 900 photos to boot. What a sweetheart!

About the Author

Diane H. Morris is a Jane girl: Jane Eyre *and* Jane Austen. She discovered the novel *Jane Eyre* when she was thirteen years old, bought the paperback with her babysitting money—it cost a mere 60 cents back then—and reads it often. It's her favorite novel. Not until she was past forty did she read Jane Austen. Even so, she loves all of Austen's novels and was so captivated by Anne de Bourgh, a character in *Pride and Prejudice*, that she published her version of Anne's story in the novel *Rosings Park*. Although she was trained in the fields of nutrition science, biochemistry, and dietetics, Diane enjoys history and is drawn to the study of the Regency era—a time of elegance and innovation, of pleasure and vice—a time before the germ theory of disease; before antibiotics, safe anesthesia, and effective antiseptics; before there was hardly any expectation that a child would survive beyond the age of eight or ten. She counts herself lucky to have been born in the 20th century and is grateful for Alexander Fleming's discovery of penicillin, which likely saved her life.

Other Books by the Author

Rosings Park: A Novel

Anne de Bourgh's character is forever fixed as sickly and cross, thanks to Miss Elizabeth Bennet, the heroine of *Pride and Prejudice*. Now six and twenty years old, Anne has not yet married and worries about her future. Her mother, Lady Catherine, expects her to marry her cousin Fitzwilliam Darcy, but Anne vows never to marry a man her mother has chosen—especially Darcy. Anne hopes to marry for love, but being engaged to Darcy since her infancy poses a problem: What should she do when Darcy jilts her for Elizabeth Bennett? She has no choice but to compete in the marriage market. A flurry of introductions to eligible men makes her wonder how she'll find a true heart when many flaws can be hidden by good manners and a pleasing countenance. Will she find happiness? Read my blogs at www.moorgatebooks.com about Anne and Rosings Park: "Anne de Bourgh Inherited Rosings Park" and "Let's Talk about Anne de Bourgh."

The *Surgeon's Duty* Series:

Ravaging the Dead

In Book 1 of the *Surgeon's Duty* series, James Hammond is training to be a surgeon at St. Thomas's Hospital in London. He spends hours dissecting cadavers to learn anatomy and recognizes the moral hazard in this enterprise. Who are the monsters: the resurrection men who dig up newly buried bodies and deliver them to London's medical schools ... or the surgeons who pay for the fresh corpses? His conscience is not much bothered by the answer. He readily pays the body-snatchers for their filthy commodity, for they spare him the trouble of digging up the dead himself. When his friend Franklin Doyle begs him to treat his fiancée's broken arm, Hammond answers the call of duty but feels a great anxiety. Then he remembers: he stands on the shoulders of giants—those surgeons who dare to perform complex operations without anesthesia, without good antiseptics ... with little more than courage and raw skill. His decision to treat the lady is right and proper, but it challenges his confidence and upends his future. Read my blog: "Regency Surgery Was Awful."

Naught but Butchers

Book 2 takes place in Nottingham, Nottinghamshire in 1817. James Hammond feels like a foreigner in this small, northern hospital, mainly because he hails from London, where he trained under some of England's most innovative surgeons. As in London, he performs dissections whenever possible, an activity that some hospital Board members and the families of some patients dislike. For them, dissections are nothing more than butchering the dead. His reputation is further sullied by the fact that some subjects for dissecting are bought from body-snatchers. When Hammond undertakes a daring procedure, his superior, Augustus Killmaster, begins to resent his looks, his training, and his confidence. Killmaster and his friend, Walter Ewebank, plot to get rid of the young, southern upstart. After

Killmaster nicks himself during a dissection, Hammond briefly becomes notorious. He never imagined that his drive to understand human anatomy through dissection would spark such shocking repercussions. Read my blogs about body-snatchers: "Body-snatchers Dug Up the Dead"and "Body-snatching in the United States."

No Hallowed Ground

The action in Book 3 also occurs in 1817 in Nottingham. Since Augustus Killmaster's death, James Hammond has grown optimistic about his prospects at the Nottingham General Hospital, but he worries about Walter Ewebank, a prominent board member who grieves for his friend. Since Ewebank unearthed Killmaster's coffin, a maggot has burrowed into his brain and will not let him rest. It feeds his anger; it fuels his discontent and only one action—revenge—will satisfy it. Meanwhile, the youth Jack Pegg continues working with Macreadie to dig up the dead and ship the bodies to Edinburgh. Pegg spends his idle hours watching the foot traffic near St. Peter's Square. He has come north for a very particular reason and is only waiting for the sign that will change his life. While Pegg watches and waits, Miss Hannah Freestone realizes that she has fallen in love with the handsome James Hammond, but she sees an enormous barrier to her happiness. Can she bury her past and return Hammond's affection or will she remain unmarried? Read my blogs about the Regency era: "Researching the Regency: Looking through Boswell's Eyes"and "Rev. Mr. Bate Dudley Accused of Crim. Con."

A list of quotations cited in this novel
can be found on my website
at www.moorgatebooks.com

Connect with Diane H. Morris

Thanks for reading *Cousin Anne*!

I hope you'll leave a review of it
on your favorite retail website.

###

At any time you can connect with me here:

On Twitter: https://twitter.com/Moorgate1812

On my website: https://www.moorgatebooks.com

Subscribe to my Regency-era blog at:
https://www.moorgatebooks.com
(The button to subscribe is located
on the homepage.)

Find me on smashwords.com
@ MorrisD1816